BEAR'S MIDLIFE CHRISTMAS

FATED OVER FORTY

MEG RIPLEY

SHIFTER NATION

Disclaimer

This book is intended for readers age 18 and over. It contains mature situations and language that may be objectionable to some readers.

CONTENTS

BEAR'S MIDLIFE CHRISTMAS

BEAR'S MIDLIFE CHRISTMAS

FATED OVER FORTY

1

"Don't look so sad now that it's finally time to close," Tricia said as she locked the entrance to Cloud Ridge Winery. "I think just about everyone in Carlton has come through those doors."

"I just hope I did everything right, you know? I've got a lot riding on this open house. I don't want to blow my chance to make a good first impression on everyone in the area." Tara Fitzpatrick-Day looked around the room. It was still early in December, but she'd already decorated every surface for the holidays. The sleek, modern winery boasted an elegant Christmas tree in the front window, and gold garland had been draped over the mantel and framed paintings on the walls. Electric candles flickered, enhancing the cozy atmosphere.

"It was fine," Shannon assured her, tucking a strand of her dark hair behind her ear. "More than fine, actually. You had a great turnout, and I'm pretty sure everyone took one of those coupons on their way out. You'll be flooded with holiday business over the next couple of weeks."

"You'll definitely have to keep this new wine in stock, though," Michelle said as she wagged an empty bottle in the air. "I'll have to pretend I don't know about it. I only have so much time to get out and have a few glasses with a baby at home, and it's damn good stuff!"

"You ladies are too kind." Tara didn't know how her twin sister Tricia had managed to make so many friends since their impromptu move to Carlton, but she'd found quite the collective of fun women. "I just inherited this place from my aunt, and I feel like I'm still winging it. I know there's a lot of competition around here, so I want everything to be perfect."

"You *always* do," Tricia chided. "You're doing great. The winery looks beautiful for the holidays, and the wine itself is incredible."

"She's right," Jenna agreed. "If this weren't such a classy place, I'd tell you to market it as being better than sex."

"It's way better than my first time, anyway,"

Shannon snickered. "I was dating this jock who'd built himself up as this experienced guy who knew all sorts of things about how to please a woman. I'm ashamed to say I was dumb enough to believe him. It ended in about five seconds."

"I don't know," Michelle replied with a smirk. "That might be better than a guy who tries too hard."

Tricia refilled her glass from the bottle on the table. "Oh no. What did he do?"

"More like what *didn't* he do," Michelle quipped. "I swear he was trying to recreate one of the movies he used to steal from his dad's sock drawer. He had me all twisted up like a freaking pretzel! It took me a while to figure out why anyone even bothered doing it after that experience."

"I hear you." Jenna drained the last sip from her glass and set it down. "I remember all my girlfriends in high school talking about hooking up with their boyfriends and how great it was, so I thought I was missing out. Of course, my boyfriend was thrilled that I'd finally changed my mind. I just wish his grandmother hadn't walked in on us. We were both traumatized."

The women were laughing so hard now that Tara

could barely hold onto her wine glass. She swiped a tear away from her eye.

"What about you?" Shannon asked. "Did you have to suffer as badly as we did?"

"No, not exactly." Tara studied the way the flames reflected in her glass as she turned the stem in her hands.

"Oh, boy." Her twin gently elbowed her. "Here comes the Corey Story."

"Ooo, sounds like a good one," Shannon said with a smile.

"You know, it really was," Tara admitted. "It was over spring break during my senior year of high school. Tricia and I had come up here to Carlton to visit our aunt, which we tried to do a few times a year. I knew I'd be going off to college, so it would be harder to come up and see her as often, and I really wanted to spend some time with her. But I had to make up for that later because I ended up spending all my time with a boy I met."

"And left me sitting around bored off my ass the whole time," Tricia added. "Then when she came back to the farm, it was all, 'Corey's so funny. Corey's so hot. He's the most amazing guy I've ever met. I think I'm in *love*.' Ugh. It was gross."

"You were just jealous," Tara teased, even though

she knew that wasn't really the case. The girls had spent plenty of time talking about that week in the months and years afterward. "It was pure kismet when we met, like we were meant to be together. I'm sure I was super annoying going on and on about him, but I couldn't help it. He was my first, and he was so sweet and gentle. We promised to call each other and try to do the long-distance thing because what we had was special. But then I never heard from him again. Even when I paged him with our special code, I got nothing."

"Typical guy, and we always fall for it," Shannon said.

"Oh my god," Michelle giggled. "I almost forgot about beepers! My friends and I never left the house without ours back in the nineties."

"Same here," Shannon agreed. "There should be a class that teaches girls everything guys say to try to get into your pants. 'I love you. I'm not like other guys. You're the only girl who's made me feel this way.' I've talked with my daughter about it a lot, but I think plenty of her friends have fallen victim to that sort of thing."

Maybe it was just the wine making her feel all cozy inside, or perhaps because it was easier to reflect on things that'd happened twenty-six years ago, but Tara wasn't convinced any of that had been the case with Corey. When he'd looked into her eyes and told her how much she'd meant to him, she'd known he was telling her the truth. She'd often wondered what would've happened between them if they'd had a chance to be together for more than just that one week.

"Speaking of men, it looks like some of ours are here to pick us up," Michelle said as she glanced out into the parking lot.

A big smile came over Tricia's face. "I told Duke he didn't have to come tonight, but he insisted. He's so sweet."

"Now who's being disgusting?" Tara taunted as she poked her sister in the ribs. "You're all mushy inside."

Tricia swiped her hand away and laughed. "And I *love* it."

"He seems really good for you," Tara said as the two of them got up and went to the doors to unlock them. "I don't think I've ever seen you this happy."

"You definitely haven't," Tricia agreed. "He's the best, and you know how long it took me to find anyone who was even worth a second date. I tried to resist him at first, but I just couldn't."

"I wonder if I'll ever have that again," Tara

mused as they waited for the men to walk up from the parking lot. "I mean, I thought I did with Clint before life and kids got in the way. Not that I'm looking, but... you know."

"I do." Tricia touched her arm. "And you will. I think we all just have to wait for the right time, even though that's the hardest thing to do."

"Hey, honey." Duke came through the door, bringing a bold breeze in with him. The chief of police pressed his lips to Tricia's before giving her a warm look. "I missed you."

"It's only been a few hours," she reminded him.

He shrugged. "Doesn't matter. You know my coworker, Landon. Landon, this is Tara, Tricia's sister."

"I can tell." Landon shook Tara's hand and paused. "Have we met before?"

They shared a glimmer of recognition. *Landon.* Tara's spine stiffened. She'd heard plenty about him through Michelle, but she hadn't made the connection. "Yeah, I think we have."

"This is my brother, Corey. Corey, you might remember Tara, and this is her sister, Tricia." Landon stepped aside to reveal a third man lingering in his shadow.

When he stepped into the light, Tara's heart

froze. Everyone else was still talking around her as they got up and found their jackets, but she only heard it as buzzing in her ears. He was older now, his dark hair having turned salt-and-pepper, but there was no mistaking those eyes. A deep brown like the darkest earth, with a thick fringe of lashes that was still several shades darker than his natural hair color. They were wide eyes, the eyes of a boy that turned down slightly at the corners, and the same eyes she'd looked into all those years ago. "Corey."

Moving the rest of the way around his brother, Corey stepped closer. "Tara? I can't believe it's you. It's been a long time."

"Yeah, you could say that."

Tricia could sense the awkward tension. "Wait, is this–"

A quick glance from Tara told her everything she needed to know.

Corey might have had the same eyes Tara remembered, but the rest of him had grown into a man. He'd been a wiry boy when she'd known him before, fit but with the slimness of youth. He'd filled out now, with wide shoulders and a broad chest. Fine lines accented the corners of his eyes, just enough to prove how long it'd been since they'd seen each other.

Corey leaned on the edge of the bar. It was a casual move, something that anyone might've done, but it made her feel like she was the only person in the room. "What've you been up to?"

"Well, a lot, I guess. It's been over twenty-five years." It really had been a long time. A lifetime, considering all that she'd experienced since the last time they'd seen each other. Marriage, children, divorce. That didn't stop the wild emotions from taking over her heart. Tara still felt the thrill of being close to him, the same sensation that'd swept her up all those years ago and made her want to spend a lifetime staring into his eyes.

Only a moment later, though, that dull, throbbing ache had once again taken over. Their little romance had been a fairytale, the kind of thing Tara had always dreamed about but never thought was possible. Then it was all yanked out from under her, sending her into a deep, black abyss.

He flicked his tongue over the corner of his mouth. It was another one of those subtle gestures that probably didn't mean a damn thing but somehow made her heart start playing her ribs like a xylophone. "We should get together sometime and catch up."

"I—"

A resounding crash rippled through the room. Tara turned to see a smattering of broken glass at Michelle's feet.

"I'm so sorry! I swept it right off the table while putting my coat on."

"Don't worry about it," Tara assured her. "It happens all the time. I've got to sweep the floor, anyway, so I'll get it cleaned up."

"I've got it," Tricia volunteered, heading for the broom behind the bar.

Tara turned back to Corey, feeling the sting of being yanked back into reality. She was standing there talking to him, a man she never thought she'd see again. How many times had she hoped this would happen? But that would've been on a random street corner, not in the middle of her winery, surrounded by her new friends.

Friends who'd just heard her Corey Story.

"Um, yeah. We should do that sometime."

Corey shoved his elbow against the bar to right himself again and took another step toward Tara. "How about this weekend? If you're free, that is."

Tara was acutely aware of all the noise and movement behind her. She heard every whisking sweep of the broom and the clink of glass as Tricia swept it into the dustpan. The other women were still chattering and laughing as they grabbed their purses and pushed in their chairs. The whole world was invading her mind, yet she couldn't tear her eyes away from Corey's handsome face. Heat crept under her skin. This was the guy who'd broken her heart. He'd affected her more than she could even begin to explain, and by all rights, she should be furious with him.

Even so, she felt the unbelievable pull she'd first experienced all those years ago, a magnetic force that made her want to close the space between them and see if his cologne still smelled the same. "Sure."

2

Corey thrust his arms up, shoving the weights into the air, and then slowly let them back down again. He clenched his teeth, trying to focus on the burning in his muscles and the thumping of his old Soundgarden CD through the clanhouse gym. The familiar rhythms soothed him in a way that nothing else could.

Usually.

Tara wouldn't stop invading his mind. Corey had thought of her often over the past year as he'd worked on piecing his life back together, but he'd never imagined seeing her again. She was a daydream, a wish, but not a reality. His time with her may have been short, but he would've jumped at the chance to rekindle things if he thought there was a chance of it working out.

He grunted as he pushed the weights up again, going well past his regular reps. Working out was one of the few things that helped him keep his focus and drove out most of the demons that haunted him. Time wasn't the same concept to him as it was to everyone else. He was only reminded of it more when he'd seen Tara again, standing there in that winery with her hair done and her makeup perfect. She was gorgeous, but she wasn't the same girl he remembered. Her hair had gotten a little darker, and she was curvier. There was something different in her eyes, too, not just the slight wrinkles at the corners. Experience? Heartbreak? He couldn't be sure.

Everyone was like that to him, though. They had all changed, and he supposed he had, too.

He just didn't remember it happening.

Someone shouted above the music, but Corey was so lost in his thoughts and the bass line that he couldn't understand what they said. He rested the weights and sat up to find that August had just walked into the gym. "What?"

"I said, how long are you going to listen to that racket?" He paused as the CD finished the last track, and silence descended through the room. A crooked smile took over the old dragon's face. "Well, never mind."

Corey pushed himself up off the bench and reached for a towel. "Don't you like to listen to music when you work out?"

"Sure, just not that loud." August, in shorts and a t-shirt, stepped onto the treadmill to warm up. "At least, not anymore."

Corey mopped his forehead as he crossed the room to his boombox, which had been waiting for him when he returned, along with his old CDs. Even the loudest, most driving rhythms had been a comfort to him over the past year. He placed the Soundgarden CD back in its jewel case and thought about putting another one in but turned the boombox off instead. August was watching him, and he didn't want to be rude. Corey knew his clanmates had done a lot to help him acclimate. Far more than he deserved, he was sure.

"You can't sweat the pain out, you know," August said as Corey stepped over to the free weights.

"Hm?" He hefted a dumbbell and curled it up toward his bicep, enjoying the burn in his muscles as he did so. It felt real, unlike the rest of the world.

August adjusted the speed on the treadmill. "You

just look like you're going at it a little harder than usual."

Corey gave him a cursory glance. He thought of August as an old man. He looked about fifty, which should be ancient compared to him. But it was far closer to his own age than he would ever care to admit. "Sometimes it works, though."

"Is it working today?"

Corey thought about that as he did several more curls. He and August hadn't had the chance to talk much, but he'd come to know him well enough to understand that he could be trusted. "Not really."

"Nightmares?" August kicked the treadmill up another notch, moving into a slow jog.

"That's the start of it, anyway. Some nights are worse than others." Last night had been particularly bad. The crunch of bone. Blood spattering everywhere. Deep growls that were so real, they'd jerked him out of his sleep and left him sitting in the middle of his bed, drenched in sweat and wondering where the hell he was.

It wasn't just the nightmares, though. It was Tara. She was a constant, persistent thought. His brain and his bear were utterly obsessed with her. His reaction to her had been strong enough that he hadn't been sure if he could keep a hold of himself.

It was the first time his bear had risen to the surface like that in a long time, especially when Corey had been working so hard to keep it repressed.

August nodded. "I get that. I have them, too, you know."

Switching to shoulder presses, Corey watched the old dragon. He'd been shocked when he'd first found out that his bear clan had accepted a dragon into the fold, but it hadn't taken long to figure out why. August was just as much of a leader as any of the designated clan members, sacrificing his blood, sweat, and tears to benefit their little community. He did that on an even larger scale as the fire chief of Carlton. It was hard to imagine a man like that having nightmares. "Really?"

"All the time," August answered with a nod. "Some of them are so real that when I wake up, I have a hard time figuring out if they actually happened or not."

Corey exhaled as he slowly lowered the weights. "Sounds about right to me. In the light of day, it's easy enough to say it was just a dream. But when it's time to close my eyes again, I start to think I might've been wrong."

"Have you still been talking to Pax's mate,

Carrie?" August was running faster now, pumping his arms at his sides. "She's pretty impressive."

"I have." Corey hadn't wanted to talk to a therapist of any kind, especially not a human one. He'd been all the more stubborn when he'd found out she specialized in relationships. Not that he expected someone to specialize in his ordeal. It would be impossible. But he had to admit, the time he'd spent in her home office had been helpful. "I keep thinking I'm making progress, but then I have a day like today, and I think I might never be normal again."

"Hmph." August flicked open his water bottle and took a drink. He was silent for long enough that Corey didn't think he would say anything else. "What's normal, anyway?" he finally asked.

Corey put the weights down and shook his arms to let them rest for a minute. He shrugged. "I don't know, other than it's not what I am right now."

August shrugged. "I don't think there's a single person who belongs to this clan who can get too caught up in what's normal. I sure as hell don't fit in, but if I stopped to think about it too much, I'd drive myself crazy."

"That's pretty much what Carrie said, too," he replied with a laugh. "I think Liz might've said something similar. No disrespect since she's our beta's mate and all, but she says a lot of mumbo jumbo about energies and chakras that I don't understand. I'm not sure if it's helping, but it seems to make everyone else happy."

"Reiki has helped many of our clanmates," August noted. "But maybe you need to start thinking about what makes *you* happy, not everyone else."

"Easier said than done," Corey cracked. "On multiple levels." He ran a hand through his hair and realized that August was right. He was practically dripping with sweat, but he wanted more. He positioned himself on the leg press. "I don't really know what would make me happy, and I don't think anyone else does, either."

August shrugged. "How can they?"

"That's exactly my point." Corey shoved his legs outward, feeling the machine's resistance and fighting against it. "I'm missing half of my life. No therapist knows what that's like, and I don't think any amount of chakra voodoo will fix it. The whole world has changed around me, and I'm left playing catch-up."

"I understand," August replied mildly.

"Do you?" Corey challenged as he let the weights clank back down before ramming his feet forward again. "No offense, but that's kind of hard to believe."

August turned the treadmill down, slowing to a walk and then stopping. He stepped off the machine and came around the front, standing beside Corey but keeping his distance. "Corey, I'm six hundred years old. I've lived entire lifetimes that humans and shifters could never conceive of. I've lived on while I've watched my friends, comrades, and family members die. I've had centuries to figure out how to deal with that, but there are still plenty of days when it's hard."

Corey slowed down and swung his legs off the machine, putting his feet flat on the floor. Part of him wanted to rage on at the weights, throwing his muscles at a problem that couldn't be fought that way. He rested his elbows on his knees as he looked up at August. "Yeah. That's gotta be tough."

"It is," August agreed, "but I've had to come to terms with it. There aren't many dragons left in the world, so it's not like I can vent to them about it. Even if I could, it wouldn't necessarily make me feel better."

"That's not much of a pep talk," Corey commented.

"The point is you and I have had lives that are

very different from those around us," August continued. "We've had experiences that are unfathomable to others. But you know what? People always think their problems are worse than everyone else's. I'm sure some wish time would slow down, while others wish they could forget half of their lives. It's all a matter of perspective, and it's only your own life that you have to worry about living."

Corey tightened his lips against his teeth. He could see what August was trying to do, but it wouldn't make his issues disappear. "I wish it were as simple as trying to think about it differently. I've probably got years and years of apologies to make, mostly for things I can't even remember doing."

"Then work on the ones you *do* remember," August advised as he turned back to the treadmill. "You can work out some of your demons in the gym, but it's not the same as confronting them head-on."

"At least the workouts help me keep my bear in check," Corey replied with a grin.

August laughed as the belt started moving underneath him again. "You're not the only one who's discovered that trick. It's not exactly easy to find the space and privacy to shift into a dragon. I'm afraid I might've started some interesting fairy tales back in my day before I figured that out."

Corey went back to his leg presses. His thoughts were bombarded by everything that had already been haunting him, only now, he had August's advice swimming around as well. The old dragon did have a point, and Corey couldn't deny that.

He'd thought the toughest part was over when he'd gone over every painful detail of his past with Landon. His brother understood what that time had been all about, and he hadn't forgiven Corey because he'd felt there was no reason to.

Many others might not feel the same, and Tara was one of them. She didn't know any of his truths, but how could he possibly tell her?

He'd have to figure it out by the weekend.

3

TARA SAT IN FRONT OF THE COMPUTER, TAPPING HER fingernails against her teeth. She'd thought out this menu, deleted the whole thing, and then typed it up again. Something still wasn't right, but she couldn't figure out what it was.

"So?" Tricia teased as she stepped into the winery's back office, carrying two coffees. "Do you have another chapter to add to the Corey Story? What happened between you guys last night? I want to know every juicy detail."

"God, Tricia, seriously? Let me get a little caffeine in my system first," Tara replied, taking the warm cup from her sister. "I promise I'll fill you in, but I've been pulling my hair out trying to figure out what's wrong with this menu. Can you take a peek at it?"

"Menu? You already did a new one for the holiday season. You're not already onto spring, are you?" Tricia came around the desk to stand behind her twin. "Um, this is all the same information you already have printed up."

Tara sighed, leaning back and pressing her fingers to her forehead. "That's exactly what's wrong with it."

"Okay, I know the winery is your thing, but what the hell are you doing to yourself?" Tricia perched herself on the corner of the desk and stared down at her sister.

Tara dropped her hands onto her lap and looked up at her twin. "It's not fair to have my own face scowling back at me like that."

"Just one of the prices you have to pay for being a twin," Tricia shrugged, taking a sip of her coffee. "Why are you obsessing over something that's already been done, anyway?"

"Why shouldn't I be?" Tara got up, feeling restless. She paced the office area, which was still plastered with all the photographs, awards, and newspaper clippings that'd been left behind by its previous owner. "Aunt Fiona left me this winery for a reason. I can only figure it's because she thought I would do a good job with it. I don't want to disappoint her."

Tricia gave her a critical look. "I loved Aunt Fiona, and I get that you want to carry on her legacy, but you're already doing that. You have a freaking wine named after her, even with her picture on the label. Everyone is raving about it, in case you've missed that. And didn't the winery just get nominated for another award?"

"A couple of them," Tara admitted. "I just want everything to be perfect. What's the point in doing anything in life if you're not going to do it right?"

"I don't know. Learning? Experiencing? *Enjoying?* Should I go on?" Tricia asked.

"That's nice and all, but I just feel like I finally have a mission in life again. I had all sorts of aspirations when I was young, and I felt like there was so much potential. Then I married Clint and had the kids, and I wanted nothing more than to be the perfect mom."

"And you were," Tricia reminded her. "You spent all your time running them to every soccer practice, lesson, and play they could cram into their schedules, and then you had healthy snacks waiting for them in the car. Just look at them now! They're healthy, well-balanced adults away at college with their own apartments. You've done a lot."

"But once that work is done, it leaves a big hole in your heart," Tara explained. "Now that you've got Duke's kids under your wing, you'll understand what I mean at some point. It's like you're so excited to see them turn into the people they're going to become, but you're also sad because they don't need you anymore." She looked up toward the ceiling, trying to blink her tears away. "Cloud Ridge is like my new baby. It doesn't hug me goodnight or anything, but I have a sense of purpose again."

"Oh, honey." Tricia got down off the desk and pulled her twin into a hug. "I get it. I'm glad you have something you're so excited about. I just don't want you to get burned out or stressed over something that's already going well. You're doing a fantastic job, and the numbers and the award nominations show that."

"Yeah. I guess they do," Tara admitted. She squeezed her sister and then took a step back. "I guess the menu is fine, but it was a nice distraction from Corey."

"All right, time to stop avoiding the elephant in the room. Come on. Tell me everything." Tricia waved her fingers toward herself. "You must've freaked out when he showed up here like that. I saw that you got to talk for a moment, but I didn't want to make a scene and ask you about it in front of everyone last night."

"Speaking of, did you have any idea he was in town?" Tara had started to pace in the other direction, but now she rounded on her sister. "Your man works with his brother, after all."

Tricia lifted her hands in the air innocently. "I'd heard the name mentioned, but I didn't know it was *that* Corey. Last night was the first time I'd met him. You spent all that time with him, not me."

"Fair enough." Tara let out a long breath. "In a lot of ways, it was like running into anyone from your past. You know. 'Hi.' 'How are you?' 'We should catch up sometime.'"

"So, he asked to get together?" Tricia was grinning now. "That's got to make you happy, right?"

Tara squeezed her shoulder up toward her ear. "I don't know. I'm not sure what to think about the whole thing. I do know I need to do inventory this week." She headed into the large storage room where the wine bottles were kept before refrigeration. Shelves with a special racking system lined the walls and formed aisles down the long room. It was a peaceful place, one that she liked to escape to when she could.

"Is this just another distraction?" Tricia asked from the doorway.

"Yes," she admitted. "But it really does need to be done. You want to grab the tablet and come help me?"

"Can do." Tricia stepped back toward the desk and returned with the tablet in her hands a moment later. "I have to admit, I've gotten used to working in the pumpkin fields, but waitressing isn't really my thing."

"Are you still wondering if the pumpkin patch was Fiona's last prank on you?" Tara asked as she stood on her tiptoes to count the bottles of Pinot Noir left. It was one of their most popular varieties, and they would need to get more out of their larger storage unit soon.

Tricia poked the number into the tablet. "I really did at first, but now not so much. I actually love it, and how lucky was I that Duke happened to be right next door? I think she definitely knew some things that I didn't. Of course, we're not supposed to be talking about me or the pumpkin patch. Tell me about you and Corey."

"God, I don't know." Tara moved down to the

next section and began tallying the Chardonnay. "I think my Corey Story has now become my Corey Problem. Twenty bottles. Put a note that we need to get more of that in right away."

"Not so sure about going out with him?" The light from the tablet glowed on Tricia's face in the dim room as they stepped down toward the Cabernet Sauvignon.

"Why should I be?" Tara flicked her fingers along the corks as she counted. "He was the most amazing thing to ever happen to me when we met. I was head-over-heels for him, and I thought it was actually going to turn into something. Then he just up and disappeared. I have no idea what happened. Damn it. I lost count."

"This would give you the chance to find out," Tricia offered. "It's been a long time. You guys were just kids when you had your little fling together. Who knows what he might've done when he was young and dumb."

"That's exactly my problem. I was wild about him then, but I don't really know how I feel about him now. It was a teenage fantasy. We're both in our mid-forties now, so I doubt it would be the same. Oh, we've got more than enough Cab." Irritated at having to count the Cabernet Sauvignon twice, she quickly moved on to the blush.

Tricia shrugged. "And you won't know until you spend some time with him and find out."

Tara didn't respond for a minute, pretending to concentrate on her inventory. What her sister had said was all perfectly logical, but she was starting to wonder if logic was a part of it at all. It certainly had been when she'd married Clint. He'd been exactly the sort of guy she'd written about in her journal. He came from a good background, had just started with a company that was already paying him well and guaranteed to pay him even more as he worked his way up the ladder. He was even handsome. Clint was steady, the kind of guy who could provide for Tara and her future children. He was enough that he'd made her close the book on those old hopes of Corey, marking them off as silly dreams that would've turned out terribly if she'd actually had a chance to follow them.

But her marriage hadn't turned out to be quite what she'd expected. Yes, they had the perfect home in a quiet neighborhood, and their children had never went without. But that spark of magic that she'd always hoped for had fizzled out quickly. They were good to each other, and she'd certainly known other women who had far greater problems than she did. But that didn't make it any easier to know that she and Clint felt more like business partners than a married couple.

Had she been wrong about her idyllic view of Corey back in the day, just as she'd been wrong about Clint?

"You okay?"

Tara blinked, realizing she'd just been standing there getting lost in thought. "Sorry. That's been happening to me all day."

"It's perfectly normal when you're swooning."

"I'm not swooning." Tara started counting again, having no idea where she'd left off. She didn't speak until she finished, just to prove a point. "Anyway, you're right about one thing. Going out with Corey would mean we could talk, but I'm not sure I need to do that to figure out how I feel. The rational part of me says this is an old relationship, and there's no need to dig it up again. But another part of me got all tingly and warm when I saw him. That's exciting and all, but I don't want to set myself up to get hurt again."

"That's understandable."

The two of them fell into a companionable silence as they continued to inventory the wine bottles, with the exception of Tara giving numbers over her shoulder. Tricia followed along behind her, putting all the information into the system so that Tara and the other workers could refer to it later. Tara allowed herself to get into the swing of her new job, which had a tendency to consume her. She had often gone to work for the day, thinking she would head home after an eight-hour shift, only to find that she'd stayed until well past dinner time. She'd thrown herself completely into Cloud Ridge and found a special sort of comfort in that. Maybe not everyone could appreciate it, but it felt far better to be productive than sitting on her butt at home.

"I think you should go for it."

They had just finished counting the last variety and were heading up toward the office. "Huh?"

"Just do it," Tricia confirmed as she put the tablet down on the desk. "You're not sure where this whole Corey thing could lead to. Maybe it won't end up being anything at all, but you'll never know unless you give it a shot."

Tara propped her fist on her hip. "Look at you being all positive. I figured you'd tell me to run since you're usually the skeptical one. You thought something was wrong with just about every man in

Eugene, and you weren't even sure about Duke at first."

A flicker of emotions went over Tricia's face so fast that Tara couldn't keep track of them. "I know. I definitely had my reservations. I was probably right about that when it came to all the other guys, but not when it came to Duke. I'm just fortunate enough that he didn't give up on me before I came around and realized what I had. You're absolutely right that I'm usually the last person to encourage someone to jump, but I've also gotten to know a lot of people around Carlton in the few months we've been living here. If they're friends with Corey—and it seems like quite a few of them are—he can't be that bad."

Tara felt her shoulders sag a little. She'd expected Tricia to discourage her. She was there to pick up the pieces when Corey had disappeared, and she was the first one to say that any guy who didn't want to be with her was out of his mind. Tara had been ready to argue in Corey's favor, but she hadn't expected Tricia to do the same. "You really think so?"

"I do."

Tara felt her stomach jump at the mere thought of spending time with Corey. She felt one side of her mouth tick up as she looked at her sister. "I have to admit, the man sure did age well."

Tricia let out a laugh. "I can remember when I thought men in their forties were old farts. Those twenty-somethings all look like little boys to me now!"

They shared a laugh over that when Carmen came bursting into the office. "Tara! Did you see it yet?"

"See what?" Alarm shot through Tara's system, adrenaline thinning her blood and making it thump in her veins. Her laughter instantly died, and she was laser-focused on her employee. "What's wrong?"

"Wrong? Oh, not a thing! I just wanted to know if you saw the paper yet," Carmen squealed, waving her phone in the air, a splash of color on the screen.

"No, why?" Tara eagerly took Carmen's phone when she handed it over. She scanned the words, blinked, and then read the article again. "It's by Jill Rodriguez."

"Isn't that the editor of the paper's food and entertainment section?" Tricia asked. "I know I've seen her name before."

"Yeah, and she was here for the holiday open house! I didn't even realize." Tara was holding the phone so tightly that her fingers started hurting.

Tricia rolled her hand through the air impatiently. "Don't make me get my phone out and find it myself! What does it say?"

Tara cleared her throat and read aloud. "When I first heard that Cloud Ridge would be changing ownership due to the death of Fiona Johnston, I was extremely worried for the future of the business. Fiona had a way not only with wine but also people. She knew how to create an environment that would flawlessly bring the two together and make her patrons forget all their troubles as long as they were at Cloud Ridge."

"I had the pleasure of attending the holiday open house," Tara continued, "and I was completely blown away. New owner Tara Fitzpatrick-Day has managed to put her own special touch on the winery while still preserving the original feel of the place. She's even created a new wine dedicated to Fiona herself, a fun red that I think would please her. You can spend your holiday season at any number of local wineries, but if you go to Cloud Ridge, it will simply be magical."

Carmen was hopping up and down with her fingers steepled under her chin. "Isn't it great? She hardly ever writes about a place unless it's absolutely amazeballs or total shit."

"I think we know what category Cloud Ridge

falls under," Tricia pointed out as she gave her sister a hug. "Miss Perfectionist over here is doing a better job than she'll admit."

"Thank you for showing me." Tara handed Carmen's phone back to her. "I just can't believe that."

Tricia squeezed her fingers around her elbow. "But you should. You've seen the proof right there. You're killing it, and so is this place."

Pulling in a deep breath, Tara let it out slowly. Tricia was right. And Jill Rodriguez at the paper was right, too. She'd done it. She'd taken a winery that she'd suddenly inherited with no notice or experience and managed not only to keep it going but to make it more successful. This meant that she had a reputation to keep up, so it wasn't like the pressure was off, but at least she was heading in the right direction.

And maybe that meant she was just as capable of figuring out whatever might or might not be happening between her and Corey.

4

"This is adorable. I had no idea there was anything like this here." Tara took in the Christmas tree farm. A small store sat at the edge of the parking lot, and a shed where the trees were prepared stood behind it. Stretching out on either side of the store were numerous craft booths, selling every kind of décor and gift imaginable for the holiday season.

"I thought it would be a nice place for us to just hang out and catch up." Corey had shoved his hands into his pockets and gestured with his chin toward the store. "Want to get some hot cider? It's the best around, and you can only get it while the tree farm is open."

"Then I don't suppose I can say no, can I?" She followed him inside, inhaling the scents of cinnamon and pine. The shop was small, but it was crammed full with jars of jam, wreaths, candy sticks, pies, and gift items. A counter over to the side offered cider, and soon enough, they each had a warm cup in their hands.

"We could head out into the field and look at the trees," Corey suggested.

"Sure." Tara walked along beside him, keenly aware of every part of her body. Was she too close or too far away? Was this as awkward for him as it was for her? In a way, it was far harder than when they were younger. She'd been confident and had the whole world before her. Tara was who she was and knew that any man who wanted to be with her would have to accept that, but she still wanted so badly for everything to be perfect. That raving review of the winery had bolstered her confidence enough not to question going on this date anymore, but as the silence thickened between them, she wasn't so sure.

"So, how have you—" she started.

"What have you been—" he said at the same time.

They laughed as they moved past the saplings that didn't even come up to their knees. "You go ahead," she insisted.

"I was just going to ask you what you've been up to." His dark eyes were warm on hers for a moment before he looked down at his cup.

She shrugged. "For the last twenty-six years? You know, not much. Just hanging out," she said with a laugh. How could she encapsulate everything without boring him to death? "Well, I went to college and met a guy named Clint, and we ended up getting married."

Corey's eyebrows shot up, and he glanced down at her hand as she held her cup. "Are you still married?"

Tara knew she shouldn't be flattered that he wanted to know. After all, he wouldn't have asked her to meet up with him if he wasn't interested in her. Still, she felt a little smile working at her lips. He could still make her feel like a teenager, awkwardness and all. "No. We got divorced almost two years ago now."

"I'm sorry." He chewed his lip as they stepped into the next set of trees. They were taller there, almost as tall as them, but still not mature enough to become Christmas trees. The farm had put decorations on a few of them just to show off their future potential. "I hope it wasn't messy."

"It was pretty amicable, thank god. Once the kids

had grown up, there was nothing left between us, so we mutually decided to move on with our lives." Though Tara had never been happy to say she was divorced, she was glad she could be honest about how the whole thing had played out. The last thing she wanted to do that day was complain about how awful her ex-husband was.

"Crazy." Corey shook his head as they moved through a gate and into the next field.

They were now in the busiest part of the tree farm, where families and couples were picking out the pines and cedars that would decorate their homes for the next few weeks. "What is it?" Tara asked.

"It's just hard to imagine you having grown children. I know a lot of time has passed since then, but I guess I still think of you as that eighteen-year-old girl. Hell, I still think of myself as being twenty most of the time." He paused as two kids in stocking caps went streaking by, racing to tell their parents exactly which tree they should take home.

"I hear you," Tara replied. They'd reached the end of the lot and turned to make their way back. "There are still plenty of times when I wonder how I'm already in my forties. Wasn't I a teenager just a few years ago? And then I look at my kids. They've grown up way too fast."

"I bet. How old are they?"

Tara smiled because the answer still seemed ridiculous to her. "Josh is twenty. He's finishing up his degree in computer science, and half the time, I can't understand a single thing he's talking about. Lauren is eighteen, and she's going to be a veterinarian. I always knew she would be; she's always loved animals. She just melts when she sees them, and I can't imagine her doing anything else."

"And what about you? Are you doing what you always wanted to do?"

"Running a winery? Not exactly." They headed back toward the parking lot and slowly moved down the rows of craft booths. The first one offered a variety of homemade beeswax candles, and the scent drew Tara in immediately. "My aunt passed away and left it to me. I had no idea she planned to do it, but it's turned out to be pretty incredible. Oh, smell this."

She held up a candle labeled 'Christmas Spirit.' Corey closed his eyes, took a deep breath through his nose, then started coughing and laughing. "It smells just like my grandma's house used to right after she decorated for the holidays. She'd put out this giant bowl of those pinecones with the cinnamon scent, and I could hardly stand it!"

"Come on, it's not that bad!" Tara protested, giving it another whiff herself. "No, this is mulled cider by the fireplace, some candles burning on the mantel, and probably something delicious in the oven. I think I'll get one and try it at the winery."

"If you want to drive away your customers, then go right ahead." Corey's eyes were sparkling as he waited for her to make her purchase.

"You know," Tara said with the heavy bag in her hand as they walked to the next booth, "it's kind of strange to do this."

"What? Go to a Christmas tree farm? We could've gone to a bar, gotten drunk, and played a horrific game of pool if you'd preferred."

She nudged him with her elbow. "You're just as much of a smartass as you always were, aren't you?" It was the first time she'd touched him since she'd seen him again. It was just an elbow, something you accidentally touched a stranger with on a train. It didn't mean anything, yet she'd noticed his warmth even through his jacket.

He nodded and shrugged. "Guilty as charged."

"Anyway, I meant it's strange to be out with you, talking about candles and grown children and my business instead of, I don't know, TV shows or concerts." They headed to the next booth, which held an array of handmade jewelry. She paused to admire a pair of earrings, not knowing how to explain how she felt. Maybe she never should've brought it up in the first place, but then it would've felt too much like what she'd had with Clint at the end. "It's not bad, it's just...different."

"You'd look so pretty in this." Corey lifted a delicate chain off a nearby rack. At the end dangled a silver heart with a stamped lace pattern. He took the liberty of bringing it down over her neck. "Can I buy it for you?"

The necklace was cold against her skin, but that wasn't what made her body clench as she looked up at him. Those deep brown eyes were like velvet as they studied her, and his hands lingered in her hair. Tara's heart surged within her chest. What kind of guy would *ask* to buy her something instead of just doing it? It was a small thing, but it was yet another one on the long list of reasons she was there. "Okay."

"You know," he said as they moved on to the next booth, "that necklace reminds me of the white lace shirt you wore when I first met you. You looked so beautiful that day."

She smiled at the memory. The two of them had

smiled at each other at The Night Owl coffee shop, and before long, they were sitting together talking. It'd been so easy, like they'd known each other all their lives. Tara still felt something pulling her toward him, but it wasn't the same. She realized that she'd discussed her past, but they'd never gotten back around to his. "You know, I—"

"I should—" he said, with the two of them speaking simultaneously once again. "You go ahead this time."

She didn't want to, but she had to know. "Corey, what happened? I know we were just kids, but I thought we had something together. We were going to see each other again and call as often as we could. Then you stopped answering my pages, and I never heard from you again."

Corey let out a sigh as he looked at the ground. "I know, and I'm so sorry. I've thought about that a lot. I just kind of lost it for a while, and I wasn't feeling like myself. I had to get out of town, and it ended up being a much longer thing than I ever could've imagined."

She took another sip of cider, barely even looking at the arts and crafts on display now. "I guess that explains why your brother told me not to bother looking for you."

"You talked to Landon about me?" Corey stopped. A couple of teenagers nearly ran into him, and he stepped out of the way.

"I came back to Carlton that summer to visit my aunt." She didn't have to tell him that she'd really come because she'd hoped to run into him. "I went to your house, and he said you were long gone."

A hard look crossed Corey's face. "That sounds about right. Landon had a hard time dealing with that time in my life."

"I can understand." Now that she'd started talking about it, she knew she had to get it all out. "It hurt me, too. I'm not saying that to be dramatic, but it was tough for me. I'd hoped you'd go to my senior prom with me, but I ended up not going at all. I couldn't figure out what had happened or why you wouldn't talk to me. It all sounds ridiculous now that it's so far in the past, but you broke my heart, Corey. Enough that I wasn't even sure if I should agree to see you again." She blinked away a glistening of tears as she pretended to look at a tiny ceramic gingerbread house.

"Tara." He breathed her name in that deep voice of his, sending a thrill through her body that she wished she could deny. "Tara, look at me."

She turned away from the booth, and he took

both of her hands in his to pull her away from the crowd, a tear trickling down his cheek. "I can't even begin to tell you how sorry I am. What the two of us had was the sort of thing older folks would've dismissed as puppy love, but it meant something to me. I hate that I threw that away, but I never meant to. And I never meant to hurt you. I was dealing with some very serious issues for a very long time. Maybe at some point, I'll be able to tell you about all of them. For now, though, I hope you can understand that if I'd had a choice in any of this, it wouldn't have happened that way."

She was a grown woman. She knew better than to swoon over a man's slick words, but Tara hadn't ever heard a man speak so genuinely. Blood rushed in her ears, and she longed to slip her fingers between his elbows and wrap her arms around him. His broad chest, clad in a deep green sweater, looked like the most comfortable place to rest her cheek. Instead, she lifted her eyes to his and swallowed, knowing she needed to control herself. As happy as she was to know that Corey hadn't been trying to avoid her, she still needed to hold back. Just a little. "That's good to know."

"Then there's something else you need to know." Corey was still holding her hands, his fingers strong and warm as he stroked his thumbs along them. "I've changed a lot since then. I'm not the same person I used to be, and I'm not going anywhere. I know I belong in Carlton. It's my home, and now it looks like it's yours, too. Despite what happened between us, do you think you might be able to give me a second chance?"

Her heart swelled inside her chest, filled with a storm of emotions. She'd put herself through so much torment over Corey all those years ago, but there was a reason for that. No one else had lodged himself into her soul the way Corey had. "Yeah. I'd like to give that a try."

"Great." He smiled as his eyes flicked down to her lips, and for a moment, she thought he might lean down and kiss her. Tara felt herself not only anticipating it but wanting it. She longed to feel those lips against hers again and see if they were just as soft and giving as they had been so long ago. Instead, Corey turned and began walking down the last row of booths. His left hand slid up to her wrist and then down again, their palms together, his fingers intertwining with hers.

Tara was grateful to have him there for balance because, after all that, she wasn't sure she'd be able to walk without tripping over her feet. The lights and colors around her blurred and brightened, and she was pretty sure she was grinning like a damn fool as she stepped up to admire the ornaments for sale. "Oh, look at that. How cute!"

"I make them all by hand out of clay," the crafter explained proudly. "That's one of my favorites this year. He turned out really well."

Cradling the ornament in her hand, Tara admired the intricate detail on the little brown bear holding a candy cane. "That's impressive. I wouldn't even know where to start on making something like this."

"Thank you. I enjoy it." The crafter turned to greet another customer.

It really was adorable, but Tara couldn't make up her mind. It was too occupied with the man next to her and what might come of the conversation they'd just had. "I'll think about it."

Having seen everything the Christmas tree farm had to offer, they headed back toward Corey's car. He paused at the edge of the tree lot, where a massive pine sat with a small fence around it. A sign had been staked into the ground just in front, and it looked as though the family that owned the farm had recruited one of their children to help make it. *I'm the official Christmas tree of Carlton this year!* it read in shaky handwriting. *Come see me light up the season at Ladd Park next Saturday at 5! It's going to be a big event!*

"I haven't been to a Christmas tree lighting in a long time," Corey said. His chin lifted as his eyes traced the height of the tree. He turned to look down at her. "Want to go with me?"

She'd seen a joy ripple through his face in that moment, and Tara had to admit the idea sounded absolutely romantic. "I'd love to."

5

"Wow. This is quite the turnout." Corey had circled the blocks surrounding Ladd Park several times before finding a parking spot, and he could tell the other cars were there for the same reason. Bundled in their most festive winter wear, people streamed toward the park from all directions.

"How exciting! I took my kids to some events like this when they were little, but it didn't take long before they thought they were too cool for it. I kind of miss that, but it'll be nice to just stand back and enjoy it without making sure everyone has kept their mittens on and didn't wander off." Tara's hand had easily slipped into Corey's as soon as they'd gotten out of the car and started walking toward the park. She was bundled up just like everyone else, with the collar of a bright red sweater peeking through her winter coat. Tiny Santa hats dangled from her ears, and she'd even painted her nails a glittering red.

Corey didn't need quite as much insulation, as his bear kept him warmer than any human would be. He'd worn a plain sweater with his brown leather jacket, content to blend in as much as possible. He could see now that his attire made him stand out, considering everyone else was covered in jingle bells and light-up Rudolph noses.

He took a deep breath and reminded himself that everyone else was too wrapped up in their own business to pay attention to him. This was something he and Carrie had discussed quite a bit, among all the other adjustments he'd had to make over the past year. The therapist had started off by coming to the clanhouse to see him, and eventually, he'd been able to go to her home office at the Two Birches Bed and Breakfast. Corey had simply been alone for far too long to know how to navigate human society anymore. The rushing noise of the crowd around him was impossible to drown out, yet he could sense every person who walked behind him. He could feel their footsteps, and it was difficult to convince himself that they simply happened to be there. They weren't after him. They didn't even notice him.

"Hot chocolate?" a woman asked as they stepped into the park.

Corey's muscles twitched as his bear surged, but he tamped it back down again as he accepted cups for both of them. He was the one who'd come up with the idea, and he couldn't let Tara know how difficult this was for him. Then he'd have to explain the real reason why he'd disappeared. Guilt washed over him, knowing he'd only told her a half-truth. He'd begged her to accept his apology and give him a second chance, but would she still be standing beside him if she'd had any clue that he hadn't exactly been honest? Probably not. She definitely wouldn't if she knew the real truth.

"This is beautiful," Tara breathed as she took in the twinkling lights that swirled around every bush and snaked up every tree trunk. The high school jazz band played classic holiday tunes nearby, and children lined up to put their letters to Santa in a big red mailbox. "I could never organize something like this."

"Why not?" Corey slid the fingers of his free hand between hers again. Did she have any idea just how much she anchored him? If he concentrated fully on her, some of the crowd disappeared. "From what I've seen, you do a great job of putting things together at Cloud Ridge. You're getting all sorts of good reviews."

She dipped her head and smiled. "You've been following those?"

"Well, I do read the paper," he replied modestly. That was true, but it wasn't nearly as casual as he'd made it sound. Corey had quickly learned that he couldn't possibly catch up on everything he'd missed since 1996, so he'd settled for keeping up with current events. The local paper afforded him a chance to do that, and he certainly hadn't missed seeing Tara and her winery in the food and enter-tainment section. "Besides, I saw how nice it looked after you had your open house."

She shrugged, making her palm move against his and sending a jolt of energy up his arm. "I get into the season. I just think an event like this would be so chaotic to manage. There are so many elements that would be beyond anyone's control, and I think that would drive me crazy. I'd want to make sure every light bulb was in the right spot and that there'd be more than enough hot cocoa for everyone. Then I'd start worrying about what bands to book and if the timing was right. I guess I'm a bit of a perfectionist."

Or maybe you're just perfect. He swallowed the words before they could slip out. It was too much, and he knew it. As they strolled through the park, admiring the thousands of lights that'd been strung up, he could sense that Tara was still holding a part of herself back. That ambivalence had been much stronger when he'd first seen her. Corey could tell it was fading, and she hadn't hesitated nearly as much when he'd asked her to the tree lighting ceremony, but part of her was still closed off to him. He didn't blame her for that, only himself.

"If that's the case, what's your idea of a perfect holiday season?" he asked. "I imagine you're probably the kind of woman who has a lot of traditions that she keeps up every year."

"Well, let's see." Tara tossed her head back and smiled up at the lights, but then her smile faded around the edges. Her shoulders dropped, and the excitement in her hazel eyes dimmed.

Corey stopped, pulling her hand gently so that they turned to face each other. He longed to reach up and stroke the line of her jaw, tracing his fingers down it to the gentle slope of her neck. "What's wrong?"

She swallowed and shook her head. "Nothing, really. I just realized that a lot of the traditions I always tried to keep up around the holidays revolved around my kids. You know, visiting Santa at the mall, baking cookies, and seeing their Christmas programs at school. It's been a while since they wanted to do any of that, but this is the first year they've both been on their own. I'll see them for Christmas, but it's not quite the same."

"I'm so sorry." The air left his lungs. He didn't like to see her hurt, especially because he knew he'd caused plenty of it himself. Hearing about her grown children only reminded him of just how much he'd missed and how many times he could've been there for her when he wasn't.

"No, it's fine," she insisted. "That's just a part of motherhood, and even though it's hard, I can accept it. Especially because I know they're doing so well. Anyway, you asked about my traditions."

Though Corey wanted to keep his focus solely on Tara for as long as he possibly could, he found his attention being drawn away, off to the right. He looked, wondering what was pulling at him so much. A group of junior high girls walked along the path arm-in-arm, singing loudly. Several adults stood around chatting with cocoa in their hands. Everything looked completely normal, yet Corey couldn't shake the feeling that he was being watched. He could feel it in his spine, and his bear swirled uncomfortably.

It was just a leftover thought from his past, an instinct that'd been deeply ingrained in him over the years of living alone, of constantly having to watch his back. He knew that in the logical part of his mind, but turning off the other part wasn't always easy.

"I know it probably sounds pretty boring, but I really love Christmas movies," Tara said, bringing him back to their conversations. "Nothing's better than curling up on the couch with a hot drink and diving into all those classics. Something is comforting and exciting about watching the movies you already know by heart and still hoping everything will turn out okay, even though you know it will."

"What are your favorites?" Corey was happy to zero in on Tara once again. He didn't even care what they talked about as long as they were together.

"*It's a Wonderful Life* and *White Christmas*, hands down. But I've really come to love some newer ones, even though I didn't think I could ever enjoy anything as much as my childhood faves." Her smile had returned, and so had the light in her eyes. "You know, like *Elf*."

"I don't think I've heard of that one."

"Really? With Will Ferrell?"

Corey felt his chest tighten as he searched his memory. He'd had one Christmas since returning to his old life, but he'd still been recovering. He didn't even recognize the actor she was talking about. "Nope. I don't think so."

"All right. Hmm." She drank the last of her cocoa and tossed the cup in the nearby recycling bin. "What about *The Christmas Chronicles*? I'm always a little leery about the new ones, but I really enjoyed it."

Pressing his lips together, Corey wondered how he would get past this. It wouldn't end at Christmas movies. This could happen between them on any subject. Eventually, she was going to wonder why he didn't know who the last several presidents had been or what celebrities had died. He had a lot of studying to do. "Maybe you and I should watch them together sometime."

Her smile widened, her cheeks pink from the cold. "I remember us watching a movie back in the day. I loved *Say Anything* and was so glad you seemed to like it just as much as I did. I don't know how my friends got sick of it because it was such an eighties classic, right up there with *The Breakfast Club* and *Pretty in Pink*. Maybe they were just tired of hearing me swoon over John Cusack."

Now, Corey felt Tara's smile reflected on his own face. The sensation of being watched subsided as he remembered that night, holding her in his arms on his parents' couch, feeling much more content than he ever had before or since. "What can I say? I could relate to the slacker who was trying to prove himself worthy of such a smart, beautiful girl."

The brass section of the jazz band sent out a little fanfare, and the sound of someone tapping a microphone exploded through the park. "Whoa, sorry about that folks. It's just about that time. I want to start by thanking everyone who has played a part in making this event happen. It's one of my favorite times of the year, and I hope it is for all of you, too."

"Looks like they're getting started." Tara tugged on his hand. "Let's get a better view of the tree."

He moved along behind her, their hands still clasped. She seemed to open a tunnel through the crowd, and Corey could feel a difference inside himself. He saw only Tara, with her dark hair tumbling from her hat, her smile when she looked over her shoulder at him. She was warm, bright, and everything wonderful that he'd been denied for so long. As she came to a stop and pulled him close next to her side, Corey didn't have to watch any classic films to know just what a Christmas miracle Tara was for him.

"And then of course there's Louise Simpson and the Ladies' Auxiliary, who have been generous enough to supply all the hot cocoa," the mayor continued. "Where are you, Louise? Give us a wave!"

The entire crowd was focused on the tree and the mayor, but Corey could only look at Tara. No matter how much they decorated the park, it could never be as captivating as she was. "Tara."

"Hm?" She turned to him, her happiness radiating.

He felt it wash over him and pulled her closer. "I can't believe I found you again. There's been a lot of time and space between us, which could've made it impossible, but here we are."

"Yeah." Her eyes moved over his face, pulling him in as she studied him. "I guess that's fate for you, right?"

"Exactly." She had no idea just how right she was. Corey had known in his heart all those years ago that she wasn't just a fling. Tara had never just been a girl from out of town that was easy to take advantage of, like most young guys would've been looking to do. She was a part of him he hadn't known he'd been missing until he'd found her, and now he'd been living without her for so long. Just as he'd wanted to before, he lifted his hand to cradle her face. "You don't know how much I missed you."

"Without further ado, we should get this show on the road!" the mayor thundered as he picked up a cord with a switch. The band started up a drumroll.

Hardly any space was left between them now, yet her body still leaned toward him like gravity had pulled her in. "I missed you, too, Corey. I wasn't sure if things would still be the same between us."

Corey had felt both his bear and human falling into her eyes. He could drown in her beauty, and he wouldn't regret it for a moment. "It's not the same."

A crease formed between her brows. "No?"

The crowd was chanting along with the mayor now. "Five...four...three..."

"No. It's better than ever."

"Two...one...Merry Christmas!"

The sound of cheers and clapping thundered around them, but it was all just background noise as his lips met hers. Tara was soft and warm, her lips velvet as he explored them with his own. Once again, he felt that hint of hesitation, a stiffening of her body, but it melted away quickly as she leaned into him. Her hands rested on his shoulders as he embraced her hips and held her close. She smelled of vanilla and tasted of chocolate, her tongue sliding delicately against his.

Corey's fingers slipped over the back pockets of her jeans and grasped her behind, wanting to hold onto this moment, but the roar around them grew harder to ignore as the crowd's celebration infiltrated his ears. Reluctantly, Corey pulled back from those luscious lips and opened his eyes.

Tara looked up at him, her lips pinkened and her eyes burning with ardor. Delicate white flakes sprinkled her hair, and more were falling. She smiled as she, too, realized what was happening. She lifted her palm up to catch the snow. "How's that for timing?"

"It's perfect." He felt the loss of her hand against his shoulder, but he still held her in his arms, right where she belonged. "Absolutely perfect."

6

TARA STEPPED IN THE DOOR AND FROWNED. HER sister had been fortunate enough to inherit the small farmhouse that came with Aunt Fiona's pumpkin patch. Tara had received a much bigger business, but it didn't have the benefit of coming with living accommodations. Tara had rented an apartment when she'd first come to Carlton a few months earlier, but as soon as she'd gotten into the swing of things with the winery, she knew it wouldn't work much longer.

The two-story Colonial Revival was far too much house for just one woman, but she'd allowed herself to think that Josh and Lauren might come out for Thanksgiving or Christmas or maybe even a long summer vacation when they needed a break from life. Lauren would swoon over the decorative newel post at the bottom of the gorgeous banister. Josh would probably only care that there was free food and Wi-Fi, but he'd appreciate having a comfortable place to crash that he didn't have to share with a roommate.

Tara loved the subway tiles in the kitchen, the tall windows, and the French doors. She'd picked a place that was stunning but could be built upon as she put her own touch on it. She'd fallen in love with it as soon as the real estate agent had shown it to her. The only problem now was that it looked painfully bare compared to all the work she'd put into Cloud Ridge. "I guess it's that time."

Since the holidays hadn't been far off, Tara had instructed the movers to stack her seasonal boxes in the rear guest bedroom on the first floor. She'd already worked a full day but grabbed the top one off the stack. It was labeled 'Ornaments,' so she set it aside until she found the tree.

As she pulled out the stand and set the pole firmly down into it, Tara thought about Corey. She couldn't help it. He'd been rolling around in her mind all day as she made the schedule, approved the payroll, and took reservations. They'd been on two dates now, which was nothing in the grand scheme of things. It was a short enough time that if Lauren had come to her after only two dates with a man, gushing and rhapsodizing over him, Tara would've told her to get a hold of herself.

But as she sorted out the longest tree branches and fitted them into the bottom section, Tara knew that Corey was different. He had been right from the very start. It was something she'd never been able to put her finger on back then, and she still couldn't. He wasn't like the other guys she'd dated, nor was he anything like Clint. There was something almost wild about him, and she could still see it in his eyes. He looked at her like she was the most gorgeous woman in the world.

And that kiss! She felt her heart thump once again as she reached for the roll of lights, intending to put them on as the branches went on the tree so they would be evenly spaced. It wasn't like Corey had never kissed her before. Hell, they'd already slept together years ago. But now they were starting over, with that sweet awkwardness between them once again.

The rest of the tree went up quickly, with her hands doing the same work they'd done every year for decades. Corey was very much a man. She knew it by looking at him, and she'd certainly felt it when he'd held her body so close to his. It made her easily remember those few rapturous nights and yearn for them again. It couldn't possibly feel the same way it did over twenty-six years ago, but there was still so much of that original Corey in him that she'd missed. Most people changed a great deal from their twenties to their forties, but for some reason, Corey hadn't.

The jangle of her phone had her nearly dropping one of the carefully wrapped ornaments as she took it out of the box. Tara whipped the phone out of her pocket and smiled when she saw who the video call was from. "Hey, Josh!"

"Hey, Mom. Hang on a second." He frowned at the screen for a moment, and then it split in half to show the second caller. "Lauren is here, too."

"Hi, Mom! I guess Maestro will be joining us as well," she laughed as a black and white cat jumped into her lap and settled down.

"Both of you at the same time? How lucky am I?" Tara propped her phone on the end table for a moment so she could hang up the ornament.

"Oh, boy. She's decorating the tree," Josh commented with a laugh.

"Make sure the smallest ornaments are at the top, the biggest ones at the bottom, and never put two of the same color next to each other," Lauren chimed in.

Tara flicked her fingers at the screen. She was used to her children making fun of her perfectionist ways. By the time they were teenagers, they would purposely tip a framed print or leave a canister askew just to see if she noticed. She almost always did, but eventually, she stopped saying anything, making it her own little game. "Hey, someone has to make the tree look pretty every year."

"And I'm sure it will be," Lauren assured her as she stroked her fingers through Maestro's fur. He rewarded her by bumping his head up under her chin and purring so loudly that Tara could hear it even through the phone. "Are you settling into your new place okay?"

"Yep. The movers put all the furniture in place, so all I had to do was unpack a few boxes every day."

Josh laughed. "Are you sure about that? Because I can't imagine you leaving boxes out for any amount of time."

Tara reached for the next ornament, deciding she might as well continue getting something done while she chatted. "I'll have you know that one room is still full of almost nothing but boxes." Only because they were Christmas decorations, which would all be taken care of within the next couple of days, but he didn't need to know that.

"Um, Mom, there's something we need to tell you."

Tara's fingers tingled with anxiety as she carefully placed a Baby's First Christmas ornament on the tree with Lauren's tiny footprint pressed into the plaster. She didn't like the tone in her daughter's voice, though she tried to keep her own steady. That phrasing always meant something bad was coming. "What is it?"

Josh scratched his head, leaving a chunk of his hair standing on end. "I know I said I would come out to Carlton to see you for Christmas, but I can't. This big tech company in Sacramento is interested in hiring me as soon as I graduate. I've got to be down there the day after Christmas for my interview, and with the travel time and everything, there's just no way I'm going to make it."

Tara longed to reach through the phone and fix his hair for him. He'd probably duck away from her and smooth it down himself, just as he always did as a boy. Her heart squeezed a little in her chest. She'd seen Josh every single Christmas since he was born. It had been a part of her life for over two decades now, watching him go from a tiny child enthralled with the miracle of the season to a teen who didn't care to an adult who was happy to get socks and gift cards for groceries. But this was his life, and she'd taught him to live it well. "That's all right, honey. I'm sorry you'll miss it, but Lauren and I will be fine."

Lauren made a face. "Actually, Mom, I can't come either."

Tara blinked, trying to keep her face as neutral as possible. "Oh?"

"You know how I told you I got the job at the vet hospital? We're technically closed for the holiday, but sick animals who need medications and wound care will be staying there. I can't get out of it since I'm the low man on the totem pole, but I also don't want to just leave them."

She could see the genuine concern in her daughter, both for her mother and the sick animals. "I understand, sweetie. Those cats and dogs are fortunate to have you. I know you'll take excellent care of them."

"We feel really bad, Mom," Josh sighed. "We both said we'd come to see you, and it's your first holiday alone."

"Single," Tara quickly corrected, swallowing and sitting up a little straighter. She'd always prided herself in teaching her kids by example, and even though they were grown, that didn't mean she had to stop. Life was hard and full of disappointments, but you couldn't let that get you down. "I'm single, but that doesn't mean I'm alone. I have Aunt Tricia, and I've made some new friends up here."

There was a chance she might have Corey, as well. Their relationship wasn't far along enough for her to say anything to Josh and Lauren about it, but she couldn't deny he'd brought quite a bit of joy to her holiday season already. The Christmas tree farm had been sweet, a nice walk down memory lane that helped her reconcile the two kids who'd met one spring and the two adults who'd met again. The tree lighting had been romantic, the kind of thing people saw in Hallmark movies that never happened in real life. She'd gone to sleep dreaming of it, unable to erase the feeling of his lips from hers and not wanting to.

Would there be more? Could she dare to imagine him showing up at her place on Christmas Eve, spending the night reminding her just how much they'd had between them before, and waking up on Christmas morning to do it all over again? It was a silly thought, maybe, but Corey seemed to make her lose some of the rational side of herself.

"I was really hoping to meet Aunt Tricia's

boyfriend and his kids," Lauren lamented. "Maybe I can come out sometime after the holidays. I want to see your house, too."

"Of course," Tara enthused. "Any time you want."

Josh looked troubled. "I don't like this. I'll call the tech firm and tell them they need to hold the interview for a couple of days."

"Don't you dare!" Tara gave her son a stern look, though she wasn't sure how it would translate through video. "If you wait, someone else might get hired before they even get a chance to talk to you. Don't put it off for me; neither of you needs to feel bad."

"But Mom—"

"No, I don't want your pity," she insisted firmly. "It's not like I'll be sitting here alone on Christmas. I've got people here, and you guys have your lives to live. I also have quite a bit going on with Cloud Ridge. You should see the reviews everyone has been leaving. The winery is practically bursting at the seams on a daily basis, and it's even been nominated for some awards. I've got a special holiday menu, and everyone is going nuts for Aunt Fiona's wine. Everything's going great for me, and I don't want you two to think otherwise."

"All right." Lauren still looked uncertain, but she

knew when not to argue with her mother. "I'll call you again on Christmas."

"Me, too," Josh chimed in.

"And I'll put your presents in the mail," Tara replied. "You should have them in plenty of time. I just want you to do me a favor."

Josh nodded. "What's that?"

"Have a good Christmas," Tara replied. "You know what that has always meant to me. I want my perfect tree and my pretty decorations and lots of festivities. But you guys will have to figure out what that means for you. So even if you're working or traveling, do a little something for yourself so that you know it's Christmas. Does that make sense?"

"Yeah," Lauren said with a smile. "I will."

"Sure," Josh agreed.

"Okay. I'm sure you guys have a lot of things to do, so I'll let you go. I'll talk to you later! Love you!" After all the goodbyes and I-love-yous were exchanged, Tara hung up.

Her house felt incredibly silent afterward. She felt a wave of sadness wash over her, one she'd held at bay as much as possible while she'd still been on the call. She hadn't wanted them to think they had any reason to feel sorry for her. Tara felt a little sorry for herself, though.

She did have Tricia, and even though she'd been invited to their place for a big dinner, Tara knew her sister would be busy with Duke and the kids. She was more alone than she'd want to admit to anyone, yet she wasn't sure what she wanted to do about that. Was Corey the answer, or was he just a dream she was still clinging onto? She couldn't be sure.

For the moment, Tara turned on some Nat King Cole, cranked it up, and returned to decorating the tree.

7

"I don't know about this."

"Just try it."

"Gingerbread? I don't think that goes with beer." Duke picked the bottle up off the smooth, wooden bar and grimaced at the friendly little gingerbread man on the label. He took a whiff at the top, but it didn't change his frown.

Chase leaned his elbows on the other side of the bar and gave his friend an impatient look. "Are you really going to tell me that the chief of police is too chickenshit to try a mere sip?"

"All right, all right." Duke tightened his grip on the bottle and took a big swig. He set it back down with a thump as he glared at Chase and swallowed. "There. Are you happy now?"

"Not yet," Chase replied with a grin. "You still have to tell me what you think of it, and you know the first sip isn't enough to make a decision."

"I think that was more of a glug than a sip," Landon replied. "He took it like medicine."

"I don't see you drinking yours," Duke pointed out.

Chase crossed his arms. "This will either be a huge hit or a total bomb. I want to debut it at one of my tasting parties, but not until a few people have tried it. My opinion doesn't count because I've already tasted it a million times while trying to craft it."

Landon considered his bottle. "I'll do my best, but I'm not big on cinnamon. It makes me think of my grandmother's house at Christmas time, but not in a good way."

Corey laughed, knowing he'd just shared that story with Tara. He took a sip of his beer, grateful that he had this chance to spend time with his brother. Duke was proving to be a good friend, too, as was Chase. The clan was more tightly knit than he'd ever realized when he was younger, and he didn't know what he'd do without them.

As good of a time he was having there at The Warehouse, his thoughts kept returning to Tara.

Their first outing had been exactly what they needed to break the ice, and the Christmas tree lighting had been a natural step from there. He'd finally had the chance to hold her close and kiss her the way he'd wanted to ever since he'd seen her at Cloud Ridge, and Corey knew what it had done to him inside. He'd found that same pull toward her that he'd always felt, the one that'd told him just how special she was all those years ago.

Now he was stuck wondering if she felt the same. He had to see her again, but Corey was fully aware of just how careful he had to be. She'd been sweet and seemed to enjoy their dates, but he could tell she was still holding part of herself back. Corey had snapped off a piece of her heart that'd never fully healed. He couldn't just give it back to her and expect everything to be okay.

"What do you think?" Chase asked.

"Hm?" Corey realized the bartender was asking about the beer, not his inner turmoil over Tara. "I think it's actually pretty good. Probably not my first pick from the menu, but it's better than I thought it would be."

"See, guys?" Chase challenged his other two clanmates. "It's not that hard to give me an honest opinion."

"Speaking of opinions, tell me what you think of this." Chase's mate, Jenna, came out of the kitchen behind the bar with Chef Drew and Amy trailing behind her. She tapped her pen at the top of her clipboard. "It's going to be easiest to stick with a Christmas theme since The Crimson Lily is already decorated that way. But I still want to go with the big balloon arch we always had our pictures taken under. This time it could be red, green, and white."

"What about gold instead of white?" Amy asked. "That might look nice. I doubt the balloon guy will have any trouble changing it."

"Good idea." Jenna's pen whisked over her notes.

"What on Earth are you guys even talking about?" Duke asked. He took another sip of his beer, frowned, shrugged, and then took another one.

"You didn't hear?" Drew untied his apron now that his shift in the kitchen had ended. "I never thought I'd be saying this, but we're organizing an *adult prom*." His forearm tattoos were on full display as he propped his elbows on the bar, rested his chin in his palms, and flashed a cheesy smile.

Landon barked out a laugh. "What?"

"Come on, it'll be fun! It's pretty much taken care of, but we're working out the final details," Jenna chimed in. "All the proceeds will go toward holiday meals for families in the area."

"You can make money off a prom?" Duke asked.

"Sure. There's a little profit built into the admission cost after the food and the first set of portraits are covered." Jenna was in her wheelhouse now. It might not be marketing, which was her true expertise, but it was close enough. She practically glowed with excitement as she tapped her pen again. "More portraits can be purchased, so we'll make a little there. All the beer will be donated by The Warehouse, and the wine will be donated by Cloud Ridge. That means every drink sold is pure profit."

Duke nodded. "I guess you can, then."

"I'm just psyched to get a second chance at prom," Amy said, who'd taken the day off from her taco truck to finalize the menu with Drew and Jenna. "Ours was awful. We'd decorated the whole gym, but it rained so hard that night, the roof caved in. The school managed to pull something together the next weekend at the community center, but it just wasn't the same."

"Hey, at least you didn't have to wear a white tux. My date was wearing a black dress, so she decided I had to wear white. It wasn't flattering, to say the least. Wait, I don't have to wear white, right?" Chase turned to Jenna, looking worried.

She laughed. "No, you don't! You just have to pick me up, give me a corsage, smile while we pose for my parents in front of the fireplace, and then feel me up in the limo."

Chase grinned. "I can do that. Especially the last part."

"And we're officially off track," Amy giggled. "All right, let's go crank out that menu." The three of them moved off to one of the tables.

"Wow. Prom?" Landon shook his head.

Corey had to agree, but he was pretty sure he wasn't thinking about it the same way his brother was. His own proms had been a long time ago, and they didn't stand out to him as particularly special. He'd done what his dates had expected, getting tuxes, corsages, and all, but they'd just been like other dances to him.

The one that stuck in his mind the most was the one he'd missed. As she was getting ready to return to Eugene after that blissful week they'd spent together, Tara had asked him to go to her senior prom. She'd run her fingers down the front of his t-shirt as she'd said how jealous her friends would be about her bringing a hot, older guy. "But the best part is that I'll get to see you again," she'd said as she rested her head on his shoulder. "Do you think you can come?"

It was impossible not to see those big, hopeful eyes looking up at him. They'd changed over the years, with experience, knowledge, and life hardening them a little around the edges, but Corey had still seen that hope in them at the Christmas tree lighting.

"I wouldn't miss it for the world," he'd told her, and he'd meant it, too. But it wasn't exactly the world that'd made him miss that event. He would've given anything to go with her, and guilt washed over him once again. Corey felt like he was swimming in it these days and wondered if he'd ever be able to shake it off.

"You know," Landon interrupted his thoughts, "maybe you ought to ask Tara."

"What?" Corey nearly choked on his beer.

His brother shrugged. "It's not that crazy, is it? You've already been out a couple of times, and every time I've seen you since then, you've been all distant and moody like a teenager."

Corey felt his face burning, so he took another swig. It turned out gingerbread stout wasn't so bad after all. "I don't know. Doing something casual, like going to the Christmas tree farm, is one thing. An adult prom is on a completely different level."

"What, you don't want to be a bear dressed up in a penguin suit?" Duke cracked.

Chase took out a damp rag and wiped at a speck on the bar. "It's not like *you're* going to look any different, Duke."

The police chief straightened a little on his barstool. "What do you mean?"

"Aren't you going?"

"I can't say I've penciled it in on my calendar," Duke retorted.

Chase let out a little chuckle. "Well, think about it this way. Jenna is one of the people planning it, so you know she and I are going. So will Amy and Evan, as will Drew and Shannon. That means Michelle and Landon are going, which means you and Tricia are going."

Duke's brows lowered. "I don't like how you just rationalized everything out like that."

"How do you think I feel?" Landon asked. "I'm on that list, too. But I'm sure Michelle would love the chance to get all dressed up and go out for a night, so I'll do it for her."

"Fine," Duke relented. "I'm not really big on parties, but you're right. The ladies will want to go. If

I'm taking Tricia, someone's got to take Tara. That means the pressure's on you."

"Thanks for the reminder," Corey returned. He drained the last of his beer and slid the bottle across the counter. "I see how it is. You come back to civilization and only get a year to adapt before everyone expects you to do all the 'normal' things again."

"Hey, we're not trying to push you too hard," Landon started.

"No, no." Corey put his hand up and shook his head. He'd had a difficult adjustment; there was no hiding that. He knew everyone wanted to help, but helping meant more than merely telling him what had happened since he left. He needed to be pushed outside his comfort zone every now and then. Whether Landon knew it or not, right now, Corey was being driven more by his guilt over what he'd done to Tara than by peer pressure. "You're right. I need to ask her."

Jenna had appeared by Chase's elbow again. "How are you going to do it?"

"What do you mean?" Chase asked. "He just has to ask her if she'd like to go."

"No, no, no." Jenna was grinning as she tucked a strand of her wavy brown hair behind her ear. "That's how *we* always did it while growing up, but everything's different. Guys do big things when asking girls to dances nowadays."

"I've seen what you're talking about, and I think it's a little ridiculous," Landon interjected. "I'm not ashamed to admit that I like being romantic, and I like to think I've done some romantic things for Michelle. But the way kids ask each other to prom these days is more complicated than most wedding proposals. It's just a dance! I don't see why I can't go home, spin her around and tip her back, then tell her we're getting dressed up for the prom."

"Well, okay. I mean, that's kind of romantic. But you two are already together," Jenna argued. "Things are still new for Corey and Tara."

Corey hadn't said much thus far, and most of the time, he preferred to sit back and watch other people in conversation. He learned a lot more that way as he tried to return to his old self, or at least, whatever version of himself he was destined to become. Things were going a little too far, though. "Does everyone know about Tara and me?"

"Remember that list I gave you of couples going to the prom?" Chase slid over another beer. "That should cover just about everyone who's in the know."

As the conversation devolved into an argument

over the best way to ask someone to a dance, Corey knew his problem wasn't deciding what was socially acceptable. It was knowing what would make Tara realize he hadn't forgotten about her, not even in all the years they'd been apart. It had to be something more than just a giant poster board. It had to mean something to *her*, but how could he do that?

In a simple question, how could he possibly express just how much she meant to him?

8

TARA STOOD BACK AND PUT HER HANDS ON HER HIPS. She'd spent every free moment she'd had over the last couple of days decorating. As soon as she got home from the winery, she changed clothes and went to work. It wasn't just about winding lighted garland all the way up the banister and adjusting the swag on the mantle to be just so. It was about settling into this new house. Some of the furniture wasn't in quite the right place, and despite her careful organizing, not every knickknack had made it to the correct location after the move. She realized she hadn't hung up her favorite oil painting, one she'd gotten from a thrift store several years ago, and spent an extra hour digging it out and putting it up so it would add to the total effect of the holidays.

Her feet were sore, and her shoulders were in knots. She was sure she'd heard every Christmas song ever written at least five times, and she'd probably missed a meal or two. As she took it all in, though, Tara knew it was worth it.

Her home now glowed with the light and love of the holiday season, just as the winery did. The tiny white lights, the fragrant greenery, and the vintage ornaments passed down through her family made her feel all cozy inside. The only thing she needed was a cup of hot cocoa spiked with a touch of peppermint schnapps and a crackling fire.

As she sat down a few minutes later, curling up with her favorite mug, she knew that wasn't all that was missing. Despite her assurances to her kids, she missed them terribly. Christmas had been all about them for most of her adult life, and it simply wasn't going to be the same if they weren't there. She could decorate all she wanted and bring back that homey feeling for a short while, but it would never be good enough.

"I'll manage," she told herself. "I've always done a damn good job of it."

Deciding not to wallow in her self-pity, Tara picked up the remote. Any number of Christmas movies would be on, and now that her house was all decorated, she could start catching up on them.

As she turned on *Love Actually,* Tara frowned. Something was wrong with the sound on the TV. She could hear the intro music of the Christmas rom-com, but something else was buzzing in the background. "That's what I get for moving to this teeny town," she grumbled. "The internet must be too spotty for streaming here."

She restarted her streaming device to give it a second chance and realized the other noise wasn't coming from the TV at all. Tara straightened, listening. She checked her phone, but it was silent. She stepped toward the back of the house into the kitchen, but the sound was gone. Coming back up to the front, Tara caught a glimpse of something through the front window.

The sun was already sinking, and it was nearly dark. If it hadn't been for the gleam of her porch light reflecting off metal, she might not have seen it at all. A car was parked halfway down her driveway, a dark shape against the pale gravel. The trees that marched along the property's edge kept the last of the daylight from reaching the vehicle, but that was definitely where the sound was coming from.

Her heart hammered, but not with fear. She knew exactly who it was.

Pulling her sweater close, Tara stepped out onto the front porch. The wreath rattled against the door as she closed it behind her, and the lighted garland wrapped around the railing was a mirror image of what she'd done inside the house. She crossed the porch to the top of the stairs, where she could see into the driveway more clearly.

It was Corey. He stood in front of his car, a boombox raised in his hands. His face in the glow of the Christmas lights was confident, defiant even. The slightest twitch at the corner of his mouth showed something else. Worry? Peter Gabriel's "In Your Eyes" floated through the air toward her, and he hoisted the boombox even higher over his head to make sure she could hear.

"What are you doing?" she asked, laughing. The chilly breeze poked holes in her sweater, but she would've stood out there forever to see this. What could possibly have driven Corey to recreate that classic scene from *Say Anything* right there in her driveway?

Corey took the boombox down and turned it off. "Will you go to the prom with me?"

Her smile was instantly erased, and her stomach

jumped into her throat. Those were the words she'd asked him, but a lifetime ago. They didn't belong in this decade.

She'd agreed to donate wine for the adult prom being thrown at The Crimson Lily, and it all made sense. "You're asking me to the prom?"

"Yes!" His eyes twinkled mischievously in the lights. "I know we never got to go together, but we have a chance again. So, will you go to the prom with me?"

Tara pressed her hand to her chest, searching for the right words. She opened her mouth and then closed it again, smiling.

"Well?" Corey stepped forward, the Christmas lights illuminating him. His hair was wild as it always was, and there was that magnetic smile. It was confident but not cocky. He knew she would say yes, but not because of him. It was about her. It was about *them.*

"A simple yes just doesn't seem like enough after all that," she admitted. "But how could I say anything else?"

"Good." His eyes locked on hers as he came up the steps. Corey stopped just below her, pressing a gentle kiss to her lips. "Then I'll come pick you up."

He might as well pick her up right now, considering he'd swept her completely off her feet. Tara's entire being leaned toward him, wanting him to kiss her again. She was going to lose her balance if she stood there for much longer, but then she realized she had her hands curled around the lapel of his coat. "It was sweet of you to ask me like that."

His eyes danced over her face, taking in her features with such admiration that she could hardly stand it. "It wasn't too much?"

"No," she laughed, wishing she knew how to tell him it was exactly what she would've wanted. It showed her so much about Corey and reminded her why she'd fallen so hard for him yet again. But admitting that to him was crossing that line of vulnerability, the one she hadn't been able to shove herself past just yet. Everything with Corey was too good to be true. She had to be fooling herself or letting herself get too caught up in the nostalgia of being with him to see it for what it really was. Every part of her told her it was true, but her mind couldn't quite accept it.

"How did you manage to find an old boombox?" she asked, knowing she couldn't just stand there and stare at him forever. "I haven't seen one of those in ages. Kids these days would have to hold a cell phone over their heads."

"They missed out," Corey admitted, still close enough that she could smell his cologne. Woodsy, with a bit of citrus. "My parents held onto a lot of my things. I thought the actual boombox was the only way to go."

"You were right." She knew she had to be grinning far too much. Corey seemed to inspire that in her. The tiny white lights surrounding them made her realize she knew exactly why she wanted to make the holiday cheer inside her home perfect. "Do you want to come inside for some coffee or cocoa?"

His gaze lifted to the porch around them and then drifted over to the big picture window, where the tree could clearly be seen. Some of the softness left his face. He straightened, creating a gap between them that was only a few inches wider than it'd been a minute ago, but it felt like a chasm. "I can't. I'm sorry. I have some things I need to do tonight."

"Okay." She swallowed her disappointment. Tara wanted him there with her. She wanted to have him next to her on the couch, watching movies, their fingers gently brushing each other. But that was something from before, the kind of thing they had time for when they were young and didn't have as many responsibilities.

Corey moved backward, lowering himself a step. He took her hand and lifted it to his lips, gently pressing their warmth against her skin. He looked up at her, still holding her hand in his. "I can't wait to see you on Saturday night."

"Me, too." Tara watched him walk back to his car, carrying the heavy stereo by the handle as though it weighed nothing. When he reached his car door, she turned to head back inside. She risked a peek through the doorway just as his headlights spun around and pointed in the other direction, lighting up the night and leaving her front yard in darkness.

Inside, she leaned against the doorframe. What a gesture! She'd been trying so hard to hold back with him, knowing she needed to take things slowly for multiple reasons. But that right there would've been more than enough to let him throw her over his shoulder and carry her to the bedroom. Hell, they wouldn't even have to make it up the stairs.

"Calm yourself, Tara. You shouldn't need a cold shower just because a guy asked you to a dance." She straightened and went into the kitchen for a cold glass of wine, then returned to her spot on the couch and turned the movie back on. She still thought Corey would be the perfect addition to her

Christmas decorations, and she wished he'd come in to spend some time with her, but at least she'd finally get to go to the prom with him.

9

COREY PULLED UP IN FRONT OF LANDON AND Michelle's house, a place he'd come to know well. Though he'd felt like a complete stranger when he'd first come back to the clan, hardly even knowing his own brother, Landon and his mate had readily accepted him, flaws and all. This was where he'd spent the most time other than the clanhouse, and it made him feel that he had a home beyond what Chris had been generous enough to give him simply because he was a part of the clan.

Michelle had traded in her little car for a mini-van. It was parked in the driveway, with the rear windshield covered in stickers that proudly declared her love for books and the middle school she worked at. Corey smiled as he walked past it, wondering how a straitlaced guy like Landon had managed to find a woman who was so sweet, caring, and outgoing.

He took out his key to let himself in, but he changed his mind and raised his fist to knock. Corey took a step back while he waited, seeing that the flowers on either side of the small porch had been cut down and mulched over. A few dry leaves skittered across the concrete behind him.

The door swung open. Michelle had baby Corey, named after his uncle, tucked under her arm. She looked up at him in surprise as she stood back to let him in. "Did you forget your key?"

"No," he admitted. "I was just thinking it was time I stopped using it."

Concern rippled over her face. Michelle might be a human, but Corey could swear she had just as much intuition as any shifter. "Is something wrong?"

"Not exactly. I just thought you and Landon should start having a little more privacy. I've been intruding over here for quite some time now." He stepped into the living room, where he could still see the remnants of the bachelor pad it had once been. The leather sofa was now draped in tiny clothes waiting to be folded, and the hardwood floor was now littered with toys and baby furniture. Landon had fashioned a bumper for the corner of the hearth out of a pool noodle to keep little Corey from bonking his head on it.

"Don't be silly! You're not intruding at all. We love having you around, and there's no need to feel like you can't come over when you want to." Michelle held out the baby. "Can you take him for a second? I need to get my shoes on."

"Of course. I just think I should start being a little more independent. The two of you have done a lot for me, but most people don't have that kind of crutch to lean on. What do you have on this child, anyway?" Corey studied his nephew's outfit. The white onesie and striped pants weren't so odd, but the green suspenders and matching tie were a little out there.

Michelle grinned. "I'm getting ready to take him out into the backyard for some baby's first Christmas photos. I thought about taking him to a professional studio, but the last time I tried to have portraits done, I was exhausted after thirty minutes of trying to keep him happy in a strange environment. I thought a place he was used to would be better. So, does this change of heart have to do with a girl?" She slipped her foot into a sneaker.

"What?"

"Your need to feel like you're progressing in your recovery. Is it because of Tara? I saw the way the two of you looked at each other when you walked into Cloud Ridge, and you obviously had something serious between you when you were younger." Michelle gave him a mom look as she tied her shoes and stood up.

"I guess you could say that." Corey tapped a finger at the top of the baby's little clip-on tie. "Don't worry, buddy. I can't tie them very well, either."

"So, what's the problem?" Grabbing a tote bag, Michelle headed for the back door.

"I never said there was a problem," Corey noted.

As she pushed the sliding glass door aside, Michelle turned to give Corey another look. "I know you, Corey. Maybe not for as long as Landon has, and I wasn't around when you were younger, but don't forget that we've spent a lot of time together recently. You've changed quite a bit since we met, but I can still pick up on that unsettled feeling inside you."

Corey sighed. "I'm going to have to tell her."

Michelle paused at the edge of the porch. She turned to look at him, tipping her head. "Really?"

"Don't look at me like that."

"Like what?"

"Like I'm your little kid, and I've finally learned to tie my shoelaces."

She laughed. "Corey, I've already raised one child, and now I'm raising another. The mom in me doesn't just go away, and I've been just as worried about you as if we were blood. I know that telling someone the truth is a big deal for any shifter."

He sighed as they stepped down into the yard. "It's not just that I'm a shifter, although that's big enough. I also have to tell her where I've actually been all this time. I'm not sure which one will be harder to believe."

"I see." Michelle set down the tote bag and pulled out a red blanket, which she spread beneath a small evergreen. "That's a tough one. Knowing you can not only turn into a bear but were cursed to remain in that form for decades."

"Don't forget the part where I went feral in the process." When Michelle took the baby from him, Corey ran his hands down over his face. "God, I don't want to tell her. I know she won't believe me. Who the hell would? I have to be honest with her about what I was like under that curse. I know I did some terrible things. A lot of it's a blur, but it's still there. Those feelings, the blood, the flashes of images. It's like I've woken up from a nightmare that I know was real."

Michelle put her hand on his arm. "Do you think she's the one?"

"Yeah. I do."

"Then just tell her," Michelle advised.

"Easier said than done." His heart clenched so hard he thought his ribs might break. "She's delicate, you know? She has this happy personality and likes to act like everything is all right. I get it, but I don't think Tara knows I can see right through it. I can sense the hesitation she feels about me. Every time she looks at me, it's like she's saying, 'I'm having a lot of fun here, but when is he going to hurt me again?' I hate that I'm the person who made her feel that way, and I don't know how to get past it."

"It sounds to me like you do." Michelle set baby Corey down on the blanket and tugged gently at his onesie so that it sat evenly across his shoulders. She straightened his tie and swiped her finger across his forehead to rearrange his downy hair. "You've already said that you need to tell her. You're right, and it's the first step to getting all of this figured out. You want Tara to forgive you for hurting her and disappearing when you were cursed. She's never going to be able to forgive you if she doesn't understand exactly what it is she's forgiving. What does she think happened?"

"I gave her a lame excuse about losing my shit and going away for a while." It had been painful to lie to Tara like that, and he hadn't quite known how to feel about the fact that she seemed to accept it. She hadn't pressed him for specifics or demanded to know why he couldn't so much as write a letter or pick up a phone to break things off with her instead of leaving her hanging. Corey imagined she must have wondered, but she hadn't asked.

"That's not entirely a lie," Michelle noted. She squatted down on the ground in front of her son, holding out her phone. "Corey! Corey, sweetie! Look at Mommy! Let's get pretty pictures to send to Grandma!"

Baby Corey was too busy to take a good photo. He leaned forward, grabbed the edge of the blanket, and pulled it into his lap.

"But anyway," Michelle said as she gently tugged the blanket back into place and tried again. "The only way you're ever going to figure this out with her is by being honest."

"She's going to freak out. She's the kind of person who likes everything just so. Everything is perfect around her. She never has a hair out of place or a thread hanging off her clothes. Her winery and house are decorated so well, they look like pictures in a catalog. I look at all that and don't even know why she'd want to give a guy like me a chance. She ought to be dating a Ken doll or an underwear model or something." He ran a hand through his hair out of frustration, but it only reminded him of how shaggy it was. Corey had been so tempted to take Tara up on her offer to come inside after he'd asked her to the prom. It was the perfect moment, and it all went according to plan. No, even better than he'd planned. Corey hadn't anticipated just how much his gesture would mean to her. That kiss between them had been subtle and sweet, yet he'd known it could've led to so much more if they'd just let it.

"Corey." Michelle was sitting on the ground now, her phone still in her hand, but she looked up at her brother-in-law. "You're right. She very well might freak out. Believe me, it's not easy for a human to understand what life is like for shifters, and your story is particularly unique. But take it from a human who's had to wrap her head around all that information. She'll get past it. She might find it tough to swallow at first, but she'll come around. If the two of you are meant to be, you can't wait around wondering when she's finally going to corner you about the truth, and you can't spend your whole life feeling like you're hiding something from her. Just tell her and see what happens."

"Yeah." The baby started to fuss, his lower lip sticking out as he realized it wasn't just playtime out there in the yard. Corey spotted a stuffed reindeer in the tote bag and took it out, shaking it to make the jingle bells on its collar ring in the hopes of distracting his nephew. "You might be right. I'm going to wait until after the prom, though. I don't want to ruin another one of those for her."

"You guys are going to the prom?" Michelle squealed. "It's okay, Corey! Show Mommy a smile!"

"I asked her last night." His body still tingled with excitement every time he thought about it. Corey hadn't been entirely convinced that she would say yes, even if he did ask her in the best possible way he could think of. Relief had washed over him when she'd agreed, but then the panic had set in again as he'd realized this meant there was a lot of pressure on him to make it the most fabulous prom night ever.

Baby Corey was truly getting fussy now. He let out grunts of frustration as he plucked at his pant legs.

"Come on, sweetie. It's okay. Just let Mommy get a few photos. Grandma doesn't want to see one of you crying. Lord knows she already has enough of those," Michelle laughed.

Corey was jangling the reindeer at him, but it wasn't doing any good. "I think he needs more of a distraction than this."

Michelle nodded. "Will you run inside and grab some of his other toys? Maybe we can still salvage this little photo shoot."

Corey turned for the back door, but then he stopped. He wanted to truly be deserving of Tara. While he couldn't change who he was, nor could he change the past, he needed to start pushing harder toward the future. He'd been hiding from himself long enough. "I've got a different idea."

Pulling in a deep breath, Corey felt his bear surge inside him. He hadn't let the beast out for a very long time. His first shift at twenty had activated the curse, the same one that had plagued the other firstborns in his family for a few generations. Living in that form for so long wasn't a feeling he wanted to revisit anytime soon. He'd avoided shifting ever since the curse had been lifted a year ago, but he couldn't just keep running away.

Pain snapped down his spine as it lengthened

and stretched. Corey grimaced, knowing this might be a long and difficult process. He'd always been told that shifting became easier and less painful the more often it was done, but he'd never had a chance to figure that out for himself. Fur bristled over his skin, and he fell forward onto his hands as they morphed into wide paws that trampled the crisp grass underneath him. He closed his eyes as the bones of his skull pulled and twisted, forming a muzzle.

He panted as he took in his new form. Corey could only see so much of himself, but he could feel all of it. He hunched his shoulders and lifted his paws experimentally, seeing that he still knew how to move in this form.

Michelle was staring at him in awe. She knew exactly how big of a deal this was. Baby Corey didn't have a clue, but he seemed pleased regardless. His little cheeks became even chubbier as he smiled, and he eagerly slapped his hands against his knees. A giggle exploded from his chest.

It went straight into Corey's heart. He moved his weight from one foot to another, making himself bob and weave behind Michelle for the baby's bene-fit. Soon, the baby was laughing so hard that Corey wished he could laugh along with him, but it only came out a breathy grunt. Still, that didn't bother his nephew. The baby continued to grin and laugh, even reaching out toward his uncle. Meanwhile, Michelle was on the ground, getting into all sorts of awkward positions as she snapped photos from every angle.

A cold breeze rippled through the yard, scattering several pine needles on the blanket and making the smile fade instantly from the baby's face. That lower lip came out again, and he burst into tears.

"It's okay, sweetie! Is it too chilly? We'll go inside. Hang on." Michelle was fiddling with her phone.

Wanting to help, Corey began his shift back. He found that his bear wasn't interested in letting go, and anxiety bloomed in his chest as he wondered if he'd be trapped in his ursine body once again. Corey sucked in a breath, determined not to live that life. He was a shifter. He could accept that there would always be a bear inside of him longing to get out, but he wouldn't let it take over.

The moment was over as quickly as it had begun. Corey quickly gained the control he needed, reining back the beast. His fur retreated, and his cheeks ached as his muzzle disappeared. Every bone and organ in his body moved and changed to accommodate his human form. When he regained it fully, he was still on the ground, crouching with his fists down in the grass. His heart was thundering, and his breath was jagged, but he was fine.

It had felt like a lifetime, but it had only lasted a few seconds. Michelle was still fiddling with her phone, trying to get the camera turned off so she could attend to her son. "Shit, not selfie mode!"

"I've got him." His entire body blistered with pain, but Corey moved toward his nephew.

A scream ripped through the air. Michelle's phone went flying as she whirled around. Corey didn't know what was happening, but he scooped the baby into his arms and held him protectively against his chest.

"Did you see it?" Michelle screamed.

"See what?" There seemed to be more adrenaline in his veins than blood at the moment. Corey's eyes darted all over the yard, prepared to do anything required to protect his nephew and his sister-in-law. He saw nothing but the bushes, a little plastic slide, and a squirrel digging through the pine needles in the neighbor's yard.

"I..." Michelle trailed off as she pressed her hand to her forehead. She grabbed her phone from where it had fallen in the grass. "I was trying to close the camera app, but I ended up putting it in selfie mode. I swear I saw a wolf behind me."

"A wolf?" Corey looked around once again. The baby had been distracted enough by the chaos around him that he was no longer crying, instead snuggling into Corey's chest. Corey held his hand against the side of his nephew's head as he looked around once more, searching for danger. A dog barked in the distance, and then another one, but he didn't see evidence of anything happening. "Are you sure?"

"I know it. It was right behind me." Michelle poked at her phone screen. "Damn it. I didn't get a picture."

"Maybe it was a stray dog. The gate is open," Corey pointed out.

"If that was someone's dog, then they've got problems. That thing was huge." Michelle's shoulders were tight and her arms stiff as she looked around the yard, waiting for the beast to return.

"Why don't we go inside?" Corey handed the baby back to Michelle so he could gather the blanket, reindeer, and tote bag. "Then we can see what photos you got of Corey."

Michelle didn't look convinced, but she didn't argue as she held her son close and trotted up the back steps. When they were safely inside and she'd firmly locked the door, she looked up at Corey. "Hey. You shifted."

"Someone here needed a little entertainment." Corey touched the tip of his finger to the baby's nose, making little Corey smile.

"But it was more than that," Michelle replied. "I know what a big deal that was. I'm proud of you."

Emotions battled within him. He didn't want anyone to feel proud of him for something that came so easily to any other bear. The rest of the clan members could shift at the drop of a hat, and their only concern was making sure the wrong people didn't see them. It was awkward to have someone patting his back over such a minor thing. On the other hand, this really was a huge step.

Maybe it meant he could take some of the other steps he'd been so hesitant about.

10

"HOLD STILL."

"I'm trying. The iron is getting hot."

"In all my years as a hair stylist, I've never burned a single client." Tricia unwound the curling iron, grabbed the hank of hair, and held it aloft while it cooled.

"That's not entirely true," Tara pointed out. "I distinctly remember a rather large curling iron burn on the side of my neck when we were getting ready to go to Great-Grandma's funeral."

"That was ages ago! I think we were still in high school." Tricia set the curling iron aside and grabbed a bobby pin, carefully arranging the curl into the updo she was creating for her twin sister.

"Maybe so, but do you know how many older

folks in the family kept looking at me weirdly? I couldn't figure out what their problem was, then I looked in the mirror. It had turned purple and looked like a big ass hickey! At a funeral!"

Tricia burst out laughing as she carefully sectioned off more of Tara's hair. "Holy shit. I forgot about that! Aunt Gertrude kept glaring at you like you were going to burst into flames sitting there in the church."

"And then she cornered me at the potluck afterward, telling me that God knew what I'd done," Tara remembered, laughing as well. "Thank goodness for Aunt Fiona. She came right over and told her sister to leave me alone and that she surely remembered what it was like to be a teenager. I tried to tell her it was just a burn, but she said I didn't have to pretend around her."

"Okay, well, I'm sorry I burned you way back then. But you don't sit still any better now than you did then, so unless you want everyone to think you have another hickey tonight, you'd better glue your fidgety ass to that chair." With an expert flick of her wrist, Tricia twisted up another piece of hair.

"Right. Because everyone knows hickeys are for *after* the prom, not before," Tara grinned. The two sisters were in the ensuite bathroom at Tricia and

Duke's. Tara was grateful for the chance to get ready for this event with her twin. It didn't hurt that all of Tricia's hair styling tools from her salon days were there.

"Do you think guys will still want to give us hickeys once they realize they'll have to wrestle us out of our Spanx to get to third base?" Tricia asked as she pinned the last piece of hair into place.

"I'm pretty sure most guys would do anything as long as they knew they'd be getting some."

"True enough," Tricia agreed, misting a cloud of hairspray over her sister's hairdo. "I still can't believe adult proms are even a thing."

"Right? I had no idea they'd become such a trend all over the country. I don't know. It's kind of sad, though, isn't it? An adult *prom*?"

Tricia turned off the curling iron and unbelted her robe. "Come on. Don't be so jaded. How many opportunities do we adults get to dress up and get out of the house for a night of fun? We don't even have to worry about our parents smelling booze on our breath," Tricia joked. "Back then, we didn't have to worry about these extra jiggles, though."

"We shouldn't have to worry about them now, either," Tara pointed out. "Considering how you and Duke look at each other even when you're out in public, I don't think you have a single reason to be concerned."

Tricia smiled as she unzipped the back of her dress and took it off the hanger. "I might after I squeeze into this number. It looked great at the store, but now I'm not sure about getting such a short dress."

"You're going to look great." Tara leaned toward the big mirror over the double sink to check her makeup. "It's going to be weird, though."

"Why?" Tricia stepped into her dress and pulled the straps up over her shoulders. She turned around and glanced in the mirror. "Okay, it covers the varicose veins on the back of my knee. Zip me."

Tara carefully pulled up the zipper and fastened the little hook-and-eye closure at the top to keep it from coming undone. "I'd always wanted to go to the prom with Corey. I'm glad I'm getting the chance now, but it almost seems unfair that I'm getting to do it in my forties instead of when I was still in high school. I would've looked much better back then."

"Are you kidding me?" Tricia gave her sister a stern look. "He's obviously into you. Otherwise, he wouldn't keep coming around and asking to see you again. He'll take one look at you and follow you around the restaurant like a lost puppy all night."

Tara laughed as she retrieved her dress off the hanger and stepped into it. She knew Corey had a sweet, boyish look to him at times, but it was hard to imagine him submitting to her in quite the way Tricia had described. "I don't know about that."

"Come on." Tricia stepped into the primary bedroom to fetch her jewelry. She looked in the mirror as she put her diamond hoops in her ears. "Any guy who asks you to the prom the way he did has got to be head-over-heels for you."

"Are you saying Duke didn't make a big romantic gesture to ask you?" Tara ran her hands down the glittery fabric of her dress. It was over the top, far too sparkly and showy for a woman in her forties going to an adult prom. Her sister had opted for dark blue, and many of the women would probably be dressed in black. But no, she'd gone for silvery glitter with an iridescent sheen that changed colors every time the fabric moved. It was dazzling enough that it'd made her gasp when they'd gone to the store, but was it perfect? Was it the exact right thing?

Tricia let out a snort. "Not at all. The poor thing looked like he might explode just from having to ask me. It was adorable, though. He was mumbling, and his cheeks turned red."

"This is the same man who helps pull people

from burning vehicles and chases down criminals?"
Tara teased as she stepped into her gown, the fabric
sliding against her legs like clouds.

"The very same," Tricia agreed with a grin as she
fastened her bracelet and picked up her necklace.
"Everyone down at the station teases him for being
such a hardass, but he's a big softie when he's at
home. Oh, that's fantastic! Here, let me get the
zipper for you."

With the dress completely on, Tara had to agree
as she looked in the mirror. The colors she'd been so
concerned about weren't going to be an issue at all.
The silver was dark enough that it was almost char-
coal at some angles, and the iridescence was subtle.
She skimmed her hands down the side of the skirt as
she looked in the mirror, and her eyes widened.
"Tricia!"

"What?"

"It has pockets!" Tara put her hands inside them,
shocked to find such a luxury in a formal dress.

Tricia's jaw dropped. "Pockets? Are you kidding
me? Our dresses never had pockets back in the day.
I'm jealous!"

"Are you sure yours doesn't have any?" Tara
asked.

"I don't think so. I would've noticed. Wait. Look

at that. Is that a seam there?" Tricia held out the skirt of her dress to examine it.

"Yes! Do you have a seam ripper or something? Let's get that open!"

The sisters were still squealing about their pockets when a knock sounded on the bedroom door. "Come in," Tricia called.

The door slowly opened, and little Mia poked her face through the crack. "Ooooh!" Her eyes widened. "You look so pretty!"

"Thank you." Tricia smiled at the six-year-old. "Do you want to come in?"

"Daddy just sent me to check on you because of all the screaming," she replied honestly, reaching out to gently touch the dark blue fabric of Tricia's dress. "He said he knew he wouldn't be allowed to come in, and neither would Mason or Oliver."

Tricia laughed. "You tell Daddy that everything is just fine, and that we'll be ready soon."

"Okay." Mia turned for the door, but she hovered in the doorway. "Tricia?"

"Yes, sweetie?"

The little girl rolled her foot on its side and fiddled with the wood trim on the doorway. "Do you think you could do my hair like that? And that I could get a pretty dress?"

"Absolutely," Tricia replied. "We'll go shopping very soon and get you something pretty to wear for Christmas."

"Really?" Mia's eyes lit up before she raced out of the room. "Thank you! Daddy! We're going shopping!"

Tara shook her head. "You'd never know that little girl wasn't yours."

"Maybe not biologically, but she's definitely mine. Are you just about ready?" Tricia slipped into a pair of low kitten heels.

Sitting on the bench at the foot of the bed, Tara strapped up her shoes and blew out a deep breath. "I don't know. My stomach is jumping. I guess this adult prom is doing its job because I feel like a teenage girl all over again."

Tricia stood back and analyzed her sister as she stood up. "You look fantastic. You're going to have a great time tonight. And who knows? Maybe you'll get lucky and come back with another Corey Story I'll have to listen to for the next twenty years."

"Oh, stop!" Turning out the lights, they headed into the living room to wait for Corey to arrive.

11

"Wow. This whole prom idea must have gone over well. There are hardly any parking spots." Tara ducked her head to look down the street.

Corey swallowed, trying not to let himself be too distracted by his gorgeous passenger. Tiny jewels twinkled in her hair every time she moved. The fabric of her dress shimmered, enticing him, taunting him with what lay underneath. They'd been together in his car before, and he'd held her close as he'd kissed her at the Christmas tree lighting, but right now, he felt he was on the verge of something bigger than he ever had been.

"That's okay," he finally said, turning and heading back to the front of The Crimson Lily. He swept over to the curb and threw the car in park, putting his hand out as he saw her reach for the handle. "No. Don't."

The December air was dry and frigid in his lungs, but it was just what he needed to keep himself calm as he jogged around the back of the car and opened her door for her. Corey reached down to take her wrist, careful not to crush the corsage he'd slipped over her hand when he'd picked her up at Duke's. He felt silly, but he couldn't truly make this night up to her unless he did everything he possibly could. She smiled and gave him that soft look, the same one she'd had when he'd shown up at her place with the boombox.

"Thank you," she said when he made sure she got past the gutter and was safely deposited on the sidewalk.

He didn't need to hold onto her any longer, but he forced himself to let go as he shut the passenger door. "You can go on in. I'll find a parking spot and be right back."

"I would've walked with you."

They were simple words, and Corey knew she was only talking about a walk around the block, but it was enough to send that shaking feeling in his stomach radiating out through his limbs, stirring his bear. "I know."

When she was inside and he was behind the wheel again, Corey pulled away and returned to his search for a parking spot. He turned down the next street and saw that the municipal lot was full, as he expected. In a way, he was grateful. Corey needed a moment to get a hold of himself.

It was the prom. Not the prom they were supposed to go to before, but a new chance. A whole new way he could not only make up for the past, but show her just how much he wanted their future together. He couldn't get to that future without telling her the truth. He wouldn't do it that night, though. Tara deserved every chance to have the best time possible. But afterward–soon afterward–he would have to tell her.

And then he might lose her all over again.

Corey headed to the left, figuring everyone else was trying to get as close to The Crimson Lily as they could. He found a spot on the street and swung into it. He glanced at himself in the rearview mirror, but even his reflection seemed to be pressuring him to do the right thing.

He tucked his hands into his trouser pockets as he walked back toward the restaurant, sucking in the cold air. If there was anything he remembered how to do, it was going to a dance that was supposed to be just like high school. That part of his life had been normal, or at least as normal as it could get for a shifter. That had been before the curse took hold of him.

When he pushed through the door to The Crimson Lily, Tara was in the foyer waiting for him. His bear responded all over again at the sight of her. The light was different there, deeper, making her look like she'd stepped out of a painting. "You didn't have to wait for me."

"I wanted to." She took the tickets from her clutch and held them up. "Are you ready?"

Corey wasn't sure he'd ever be ready, but he nodded and held out his elbow. "Whenever you are."

The Crimson Lily had transformed from an upscale restaurant to a ballroom, all decked out for the holidays. The dining room was already crowded with partygoers, the men in sharp suits or tuxes, the women in dresses of every color and shape. A giant balloon arch had been constructed in the corner, just as they'd discussed that day at The Warehouse. The flash of the photographer's camera illuminated the room periodically, mixing with the twinkling lights. Poinsettias sat on every table, and a Christmas tree stood next to the bar. The potted trees that usually clustered around the tables to offer privacy had been pushed back against the walls, each decorated with lights and ornaments.

"There's Tricia and Duke," Tara noted, seeing the couple at a table near the corner. "Do you mind if we sit with them?"

"That would be fine." Of course, he'd much rather be somewhere alone with her, but this wasn't about him. Corey placed his hand on the small of her back to escort her through the narrow aisle to the table.

"Isn't this incredible?" Tricia asked as they sat down. "It's just like high school, but a lot classier. And Christmassy, of course." She flicked the petal of the poinsettia on their table.

"I love it," Tara breathed, making her gown shift around her again and reminding Corey of just how attuned he was to her right now. "I wasn't sure how it would turn out, but it's great. And they were actually able to create a dance floor over there."

Corey looked where she pointed, seeing that the tables had been completely cleared from the back of the room.

"I'm going to need a drink or two before I'm ready to get out on the dance floor," Duke commented.

That sounded like a great idea to Corey, and he

turned to his date. "What can I get you?"

"Oh." She blushed and smiled, and he noticed the tiny flecks of glitter in her makeup. "Since all the wine here is from Cloud Ridge, you can get me a glass of anything. I'm pretty much guaranteed to like it."

"I'll be right back." He kept himself from racing away from the table, but barely. Corey yanked at his collar, wishing it wasn't so tight. If Jenna was hoping to raise money off the bar, she'd be pleased based on the number of people trying to get a drink. Corey stepped up to an empty space and waited.

He drummed his fingers on the bar as a movement through the window caught his eye. Corey turned to get a better look, but he saw nothing but cars driving by. He purposely turned away, wondering when he'd stop having experiences like this.

"Well, well. It turns out you clean up pretty nicely."

He turned to see Landon at his elbow, dressed in a tux. "So do you, brother."

Landon shrugged. "I already spend all day in uniform, so I guess it's not much of a transition. I would've just worn a suit, but once I saw how fancy Michelle was going to dress, I figured I'd better play it safe." He gestured over his shoulder where Michelle was laughing with Shannon and the staff from The Warehouse.

"How about you?" Landon asked. "Things going okay?"

"As well as they can." Corey let out a long breath. "I just need everything to go right."

"It will. What can really go wrong? You buy her a drink, get out on the dance floor a few times, and make sure you tell her how hot she looks. It's pretty standard for us guys when it comes to this stuff. Oh, and if another woman is wearing the same dress, tell her she looks way better in it."

"I'm sure it'd be the truth anyway," Corey replied, resisting the urge to look back at Tara just to see how that dress flattered her figure. "All of that is great, but it doesn't seem like enough. I have a lot to make up for. White wine, please," he said when the bartender gave him an inquiring look.

"Just relax. Be yourself. You brought her here, and you know that's what she wanted. The rest of it doesn't have to be that hard."

Corey raised an eyebrow. "As I recall from the stories you've told me, things weren't exactly easy between you and Michelle at first. I think you're only saying that because it's easy now."

"Well, it is. And maybe it did take some work to get there, but the point is that you guys can, too. Now go on, and do everything your gut is telling you to. Wait, not everything. We'd all get in trouble if we did that," Landon grinned.

It wasn't terrible advice, Corey knew. He'd already done a lot to let Tara know just how much she meant to him, and she seemed happy. But it had to be more. It would never be enough. He made a quick stop before he headed back to their table.

"Here you go," he said when he returned, "but you may not have much time to drink it."

"Why is that?"

Corey held out his hand. "Can I have this dance?" he asked just as the poppy dance tune faded out and the first few notes of a familiar song played through the PA system.

Tara's eyes lit up as she took his hand. "I haven't heard this song in forever."

"It was one that I remembered you liked," Corey explained.

"Showoff," Duke grumbled, and Tricia punched him in the arm.

They made their way out to the dance floor, and he pulled her into his arms. "As I Lay Me Down" by Sophie B. Hawkins flooded over them. She laid her left hand on his shoulder as he took her right one in his own, her fingers slipping through his and sending a shiver of excitement down his spine.

"I can't believe you remember this," she said after she'd listened to the lyrics for a moment. "I loved this song even before I met you. I admit it made me think of you a lot after I had to leave Carlton, though."

If she could only know the pain her comment shot through his heart. She hadn't hurt him on purpose; anything they shared right now just couldn't be isolated from his past. He couldn't escape that so easily, but he could take the first step. Tonight wasn't the time to tell her all of his truths, but the drinks, dancing, and festive lights still weren't enough.

"Tara, I can't tell you how sorry I am that I messed everything up between us back then," he began, pulling his left hand with her fingers still entwined against his chest. "You meant so much to me, and I can see now that I made you feel as though you didn't. I wish I could go back and change the way things went."

Her thumb gently stroked his tuxedo jacket. "You've already apologized, Corey. You don't have to keep doing it."

"But I feel like I do," he replied honestly. The guilt was so strong in him that it was overwhelming at times. Maybe it would be better once she knew the whole story, and he could keep his faith in that for now, but it was only a temporary fix until the entire truth came to light. "I hurt you, Tara. It's hard to live with that."

"Corey." She pulled herself closer, looking up into his eyes. "It wasn't your fault. You had some things to deal with, and that's how life goes sometimes. Everyone has their issues they have to work through."

"But—"

"No, listen," she insisted. "If we still managed to find each other, even after all this time when we could've ended up anywhere, then maybe this was how it was meant to happen. Who knows how we would've been together when we were so young and thought we knew everything? I might've used up all my time with you before I could really appreciate it."

"That's an interesting way to think about it." Corey had been looking at their relationship in terms of all the time they'd lost, but Tara had found a way to turn it around and make it seem like the best thing that could've happened.

She shrugged a little, which made her breasts

press against him. "As I was getting ready tonight, I thought about how weird it was that I didn't get to have my prom date with you until I was in my forties. It felt almost unfair. But even though I was crazy about you, I don't know if I would've appreciated you the way I do now."

"Tara." He shook his head, wondering how he could possibly be lucky enough to have someone so willing to look over his flaws. He didn't deserve her. She had accepted his lie of omission, and she should be with someone far better than him, someone who hadn't hurt her the way he had. Someone who hadn't been cursed to live as a feral bear, committing whatever atrocities he may have along the way.

He was just about to tell her that when a curl escaped her updo and drooped down next to her cheek. Tara frowned as she lifted her hand from his chest to pick it up. "Oh, great. I've got to go find Tricia."

But Corey wasn't ready to let go of her. He would probably be forced to soon enough when she realized just how low she'd stooped by even considering him. For now, he wanted her in his arms as much as possible. "I can get it."

"Are you sure?"

He wasn't. Not at all. Corey didn't know a damn

thing about hair, and he sure as hell didn't know how Tara or any other woman managed to create the fancy styles they all wore that night. He could, however, see that one of the jeweled pins had come loose. He gently pulled the pin out, grateful everything didn't come tumbling down into his hands, although he would've gladly run his hands through those dark waves. Corey carefully pinned the curl back in place. "There. I think I got it."

"Thank you." She smiled and stepped back into his embrace.

"You don't want to go check it in the mirror or anything?" he teased. "There's no telling what I've done."

"I'm sure it's just fine."

The song switched, and Toni Braxton's "Un-Break My Heart" had several more couples stepping onto the floor.

Corey pulled her close, wrapping his arms around her all the way. Tara slipped her hands up and around his shoulders, and their foreheads pressed together. He closed his eyes, wanting to hold onto this moment as long as possible.

12

"It was a lovely night." Tara felt like a teenager so much of the time she was with Corey, and that night was no exception. The experience at the prom made her want to stay up late all night giggling with Tricia about how cute all the guys looked and how sweet Corey had been.

Except that now they were at her house. He'd walked her to the door, and no one was there to flicker the porch light at them.

"Do you want to come in for a bit?" she asked shyly. He had turned her down before.

But Corey smiled. "Sure."

"I'll make some coffee." Nervously, she dropped her clutch on the side table and charged toward the kitchen. "Make yourself at home."

Out of his sight, Tara forced herself to take a deep breath. What was it that this man did to her? Why did he have such a hold over her that she got nervous just about having him in her living room? It shouldn't matter. They were both adults, and they'd been holding each other all night as they danced. She snagged the pot off the coffee maker and took it over to the sink.

"Is there anything I can do to help?"

Tara turned around. Corey stood there in her kitchen doorway. His bowtie was hung around his collar and his tux jacket was open, but he still looked as ruggedly handsome as ever. Cold water spilled over her hand as she realized she'd overfilled the pot, and Tara quickly shut off the tap.

"Everything okay?" He was closer now, and he'd grabbed a towel from one of the drawer handles to catch the water that sloshed on the counter before it could drip down. When he laughed, she felt a shiver of pleasure go up her spine. "The coffee's not worth ruining your dress for."

She set the pot on the counter, a hard clunk. "It's no trouble. I'm sure you want a cup."

"And what do *you* want?" His hand lingered casually on the back of her dress as he leaned over to hang the wet towel over the sink divider.

Tara felt the edges of the room fade away as her focus zeroed in on him. "I don't want this night to end." Grabbing the two ends of his bowtie, she pulled him down and pressed her lips against his.

Corey's body tensed in surprise, but he got past it quickly. He grabbed her by the waist and yanked her forward, letting her feel the length of his body against hers. Clearly, he didn't want the night to end, either.

"Tara." He held her so tightly, and every tiny movement of his lips grazing over her skin sent a tingling shock of excitement through her. "You have no idea how much I've missed you."

She knew she could leave it at a kiss. They'd already shared one on one of their previous dates, and he was gentlemanly enough not to press her. But Tara didn't want to. She'd been holding back for so long, caught up on events that had happened decades ago. It was time to go all in, jump in with both feet, and see where she landed instead of mapping out every careful move. Pulling back but hungry for more, she grabbed his hand and led him out of the kitchen and into the bedroom.

Flicking on the small lamp in the corner gave her just enough light to see his eyes, watching her with amusement. "I've missed you, too."

They came together in a kiss once again, but this time, his fingers slipped one strap of her dress off her shoulder. Corey reached around behind her to find the zipper. "I love this dress on you," he murmured, "but I think I'll like it even better off of you."

The formal wear made it more difficult, but Corey managed to take the zipper all the way down to her ass. Tara's fingers fluttered around the placket that hid his shirt buttons, but once she found the first one, the rest were easy. The silvery fabric of her dress slithered to the floor. Tara felt a moment of awkwardness when she realized her shapewear had been revealed, but Corey was too busy undoing his cufflinks to notice her wiggling out of it.

When a pile of gorgeous fabrics had formed on the floor, Tara had a moment to take him all in. He was even sexier than she remembered. Salt and pepper hairs curled on his wide chest and trailed downward, bringing her eyes along with it. She'd gotten a moment to catch him in his boxer briefs, which stretched deliciously over his rock-solid erection and muscular thighs. But now she could see all of him, and he was more than ready for her.

"You're unbelievably hot." His voice was husky and deep, enough to make her nipples harden for more reasons than the cold air outside. He took two steps to get to her and swept her hair back with his hand, grabbing it in a knot as he kissed her thoroughly. He didn't break their liplock as he scooped his arms under her backside and lifted her from the floor, carrying her to the bed.

Desire ripped through her when he sat down with her straddling him, and she could feel his hardness against her. Being with him like this was completely new, yet familiar, and that only drove her more. His hands whisked over the curves of her thighs and hips, sending trails of exquisite magic up her spine as she lowered herself onto him.

She gasped as she held him within her depths. His fingers kneaded the soft flesh at her hips as he dropped kisses over her breasts and neck. Every sensation was enhanced as she pulsed against him, their needs feeding each other. Corey's attentions made her aware of every curve of her body because of the way he delighted in them, growling with pleasure as he explored.

For once, she closed her eyes and allowed herself to just feel. She found the strength and beauty in her body that she didn't always pay attention to. Tara had thought she'd been exercising great self-control by holding back with Corey, but as her hips moved to the rhythm of his, she realized she'd only been denying herself. She luxuriated in the thick curls of his chest hair, his muscular arms, the strength of his hips, and the deep moans that emanated from his throat. He was magnificent, and the fact that he wanted her made her skin heat and her breathing grow shallow. Corey's hips rose up to meet hers. She braced her hands against his chest, and he held onto her hips as they flew together through this writhing blizzard they'd created. Explosions moved through her body, tensing her muscles and filling her head with a sweet dizziness. They held each other tightly as they fell over the edge, with the winter wind trembling against the windows.

13

COREY SAW THE MESSAGE ON HIS PHONE AND SIGHED. He'd just gotten back to the clanhouse after a long and blissful night, one that he wouldn't give back for anything, but the only thing he wanted to do right now was sleep.

As he started the shower, he realized he probably wouldn't sleep well anyway. Tara had let down that last wall that'd been holding her back. It wasn't just that they'd slept together. He'd seen it in the way her eyes had changed, and his bear had sensed it. She'd been reserved toward him, and rightfully so, but last night she'd thrown caution to the wind.

Scrubbing shampoo through his hair, he wondered if it'd been the prom itself, his apology, or the way it felt as they'd held each other so closely on the dance floor. Maybe it wasn't just one thing. Maybe she'd had enough time to realize he wouldn't run off again, just as he'd promised. He grabbed the soap, knowing it didn't matter why she'd changed her mind, only that she had—and that he didn't deserve anything she'd decided to give him.

Not that he was complaining. The way she'd felt naked in his arms had been even better than how she'd felt in that slinky dress. She was just as incredible as he'd remembered, though more experienced now. Corey had reveled in the feeling of her soft hair against his skin, her breasts pushing against his ribs, her legs sliding against his. The only downside was knowing it would probably never happen again. She wouldn't dare touch him once she knew of the beast he truly was.

Now dressed, Corey headed down the hallway. The smell of cooking drifted toward him, and his stomach growled. When he turned the corner, he found Tyler in the kitchen, scarfing down a bacon sandwich.

"There's more if you want some." The clan beta gestured toward the plate of bacon. "I've got to get downstairs, but I had to get a bite to eat first."

Corey smiled, knowing the feeling. Anyone who stayed at the clanhouse had open access to the kitchen, and he'd taken advantage of it plenty of times. He'd come out of his feral state with a ravenous appetite, and all the time he spent in the gym had only kept that cycle going. "I'll get something later. I want to see what this is all about first."

Tyler's face darkened, signifying he not only knew what it was about but didn't like it. "Suit yourself, but you know how these meetings can go. If someone gets talking, it could be a while before you get a chance to eat again."

"Yeah. Maybe you're right." Corey didn't want to even think about food. Nothing seemed more important than Tara. Not breakfast, and not this emergency meeting. But he made a couple pieces of toast and a quick sandwich before going down to the meeting room.

The Thompson clan maintained a large house with enough room for the Alpha and his family, a meeting space, and accommodations for those in need. Right now, Corey was one of them. Chris had opened the clanhouse to him as soon as he'd returned to himself, and he'd grown accustomed to moving around the spacious house. He nodded to a few other clan members as he found a seat near the back. He slumped down into the folding chair and shoved his hands into his jacket pockets, waiting for this to be over with so he could go to bed and dream about Tara.

The chairs around him filled up quickly with shifters rubbing their eyes and yawning. Brandy had placed a big carafe of coffee on one of the side tables, and quite a few stopped there as well. Corey thought about it, but he didn't want anything to ruin his chance of sleeping once this was all over with.

"Did you go to the prom?" he heard someone ask.

"Yeah. It was okay. At least it'll help feed people who need it," their neighbor replied.

"So, what was wrong?"

"It was just like my high school prom. My date got all pissed off by the end of the night."

Their friend snickered. "Sounds like maybe it's you."

Corey allowed himself a smile, but then he snapped to attention when he saw Chris step up to the front of the room. The Alpha waited patiently for the crowd to silence, which happened quickly.

"Thank you. I first want to apologize. I know that having an emergency meeting the night after many of you were at the prom is an inconvenience, at the least. But I'm sure you'll come to see that I've gathered you here for a good reason. I will, however, try to keep this as brief as possible."

"Must be pretty damn important if he doesn't even have his notes with him," the person behind Corey commented. "I never see him without his notes."

Corey raised his eyebrows. They might be making fun of Chris in a way, but they were right. He blinked and decided he might want to pay a little more attention.

"We've been getting reports of a wolf in the area lately," Chris began. "It's not unheard of for wildlife to come within city limits, and if this were something as simple as that, I wouldn't be bothered in the least. This seems to be a rather large wolf, though. Large enough that we're fairly certain it's not a wild one, but a shifter."

A few whispers rippled through the crowd.

"Now, that doesn't necessarily mean much," Chris continued. "There are several packs relatively close by. We've never had any issues with them, but we still don't see many of them in our midst."

"Is this wolf doing anything specific or sticking to a certain area?" Pax asked.

"It hasn't attacked anyone that we're aware of. Neither does it seem to be sticking to a certain part of town. It's been seen on the outskirts as well as downtown, and it was even seen not far from The Crimson Lily last night," Chris admitted.

This caused another murmur through the crowd.

"Yes," the Alpha said, seeing how his clanmates were reacting. "It seems a little strange. While it hasn't been harming anyone, everyone who sees it seems to have a bad feeling about it. That means something to me. If anyone has seen this wolf and hasn't told me about it, then I need to know."

Corey lifted his hand.

Chris pointed to him.

"I was at Michelle and Landon's house about a week ago or so. She swore she saw a wolf while we were in the backyard. I didn't think anything about it because I didn't see it. I looked all around, and everything was fairly quiet except for a few dogs barking in the distance. I wish I had more information, but I thought I should let you know."

Chris nodded. "Every bit helps while we try to figure this out. If this wolf is here for a reason, the sooner we understand it, the better. I want everyone to keep their eyes peeled. If you see the wolf, call the clanhouse immediately. I'll send someone out right away if you feel you might be threatened. Are there any questions?"

No one had much to say, but by the time the meeting was dismissed and Corey was heading back up to his room, he had plenty of questions of his own. A random wolf in town shouldn't bother him that much. He knew now that he could shift back and forth, so he would be fine should the need arise to defend himself. Not that he would want to rely on that, but he could if he had to. Chris was a bit worked up about it, but Corey knew the Alpha always liked to take the safe route when it came to his clan.

Flashes from his past crept into his vision. Blood and teeth, howls and groans. His heart hammered as though he were back there again. Most of it didn't make any sense. It was as if his mind had tried so hard to distance itself from that time, it had eliminated some of his memories. But nothing could stop the way it felt. His gut clenched as more of his usual flashes came, and victory washed over him as he stepped forward to look over the edge of a cliff. A wolf lay there, blood streaming from its mouth.

Blinking, Corey realized he was leaning against the wall in the hallway. He straightened and looked around, but no one had come by to see his strange antics. He made it the rest of the way into his room and locked the door.

Kicking off his shoes and removing his clothes, Corey fell into bed. He buried himself in the covers and pillows, seeking the comfort of the life he'd come to know since the curse had been lifted. His brow creased as he focused on Tara. Thoughts of her were tortuous, as well, but in a completely different way.

He shoved aside the image of the dead wolf, not knowing what it meant and preferring not to find out. Tara. Only Tara. In that alluring dress, with her arms around him and her forehead pressed against his while an old familiar song about staying together despite all odds played around them. He'd been able to drown out the rest of the room while he'd been with her, and as they held each other, Corey had finally been able to stop thinking about whether or not he was making this the perfect night for Tara. Perhaps because he knew it was already perfect, simply by the two of them being together. That's how it made him feel, anyway.

The wolf image flashed in his mind again, making him clench his jaw. He rolled away from the window to combat what little light streamed through the thick curtains and forced his thoughts back. Tara, with every inch of her skin bare to him, his fingers smoothing over its surface and wanting to explore every inch. Her eyes watching his, no longer wondering or waiting, no longer holding back.

"Fuck." Corey slammed his fist into the pillow and rolled onto his back. He was trying so hard to focus on his life with Tara but those images that kept creeping in reminded him not only of his murky, troubled past, but how it could destroy any hope of a future with her. There wouldn't be any sleeping for him today.

Getting up, he tossed his clothes back on. He needed to get down to the gym and think.

14

"Welcome to Cloud Ridge. May I get you started with a glass of wine?"

Tara hummed to herself as she listened to the now-familiar sounds of work around her. There was plenty to be done, as there always was. But she found she had less to worry about today. The wait-staff she employed was excellent. Customers were greeted right away but were still given plenty of time to look over the menu. All employees knew the wines by heart and could easily help a guest pick which one they wanted to try or decide what variety would make the best gift. People came and went at the tables and the bar, and the gift area had been doing solid business throughout the day. The place was buzzing.

So was her body. Tara couldn't shake her thoughts of Corey. As she glanced over the ad campaign that had to be sent to the radio station, she remembered the way he'd looked under the Christmas lights on her porch after asking her to go to the prom. While jotting down the requested time off for an employee, she could still feel his arms around her as they swayed on the dance floor. Songs from the night echoed in her head, making Tara completely space out as she sat behind her desk. By the time she remembered what she was doing, she'd reached the most memorable part of the night.

The two of them, together in her bed. If only the eighteen-year-old version of herself could know that a warm, sweet spring could become a hot, sexy winter years later. She could still feel the heat of Corey against her, and she longed to experience it again. It had been just as good as she'd expected it to be. No, better. Because now there were fewer questions between them, and they no longer had the pressure of deciding the rest of their lives. They could take things slowly while figuring it out, and they could enjoy the hell out of each other in the meantime.

"Tara? Are you okay?"

She swirled around in her desk chair to see

Carmen standing in the office doorway. "Of course. Why do you ask?"

"I said your name like three times, and you didn't answer." The young waitress stepped into the room. Her dark red hair was bound into a braid to keep it out of her way while she worked, and the burgundy button-down shirt that was part of the Cloud Ridge uniform was just as neat and crisp as when she'd shown up for her shift.

"I'm sorry. I must not have heard you. I've had a lot on my mind." Tara gestured vaguely at her computer, but she knew her thoughts didn't have a damn thing to do with payroll or email marketing.

"I'd say. You've seemed pretty distracted all day. You had me kind of worried about you." Carmen frowned as she stepped a little closer to her boss. "Are you feeling feverish? Your cheeks are flushed."

She was feverish all right, but not because of an illness. "I'm fine, really. I didn't mean to worry you, but you don't have to act like the mother hen. That should be my job. Now, what did you need me for?" Tara put her hands together and leaned forward, forcing herself to concentrate. Cloud Ridge deserved to be run by someone who was paying attention.

"I was just coming to tell you I'm going on my

break. You said you'd be covering the bar since Dustin isn't here today. If you need me to stay, though..."

"No, no." Tara was on her feet in an instant. She couldn't blame herself for getting so lost in chapter two of her Corey Story, but work was important, too. "I'm coming. You do what you need to do. I won't have anyone saying I don't give my employees the breaks they deserve."

"I wouldn't say that, anyway," Carmen reminded her with a smile. "I like my job here."

"And I'd like to keep it that way. I've got this taken care of, so you can head out." Tara tied on a half-apron and stepped out behind the bar.

She smiled as she looked over the dining area of Cloud Ridge. There was much more to the winery, although this was the space that most of her customers saw. Tara knew there were acres of vines, two large buildings that housed all of the wine-making equipment, and quite a bit of storage. All of that was important, but seeing what she did there was the part that made her heart so happy. It was the smiling faces of a couple sitting in the corner, whispering and laughing as though no one knew they were making innuendos about what they'd do later that night. It was the group of girlfriends planning a bachelorette party a bit too loudly, and the group of senior ladies at the table nearby who giggled and reminisced while they eavesdropped. People came there to eat and drink, but Tara liked to think they were finding so much more. They would be closing soon, leaving the place empty for the night, but she was content to know it would fill up again the next day.

She had just finished giving the bar a detailed wipe down when she heard the door open. People came in and out all the time, so this wasn't unusual, but something made her look up. Dark eyes met hers, and her body began buzzing all over again as she watched Corey walk up to the bar. "Hi."

"Hey." His gaze moved over her face for a moment, looking like he was deciding something. "Would you mind if I sat down and had a drink?"

"Of course not." Tara gestured at the open seat in front of her and grabbed one of their mini menus for the bar. "We're going to be closing soon, but there's time for a last call or two. What can I get you?"

He waved his hand at the small card. "I keep hearing about this wine named after your aunt."

"One glass of Fiona's Special, coming right up." Tara pulled a bottle from the fridge and uncorked it, glad there wasn't one open yet. The first glass was always the best, and she wanted to make a good impression on Corey. Her fingers shook slightly, and she gripped the bottle a little more tightly as she poured, hoping he wouldn't notice.

"Thank you." He took a sip. "You know, I'm not much of a wine person, but this is pretty good."

Tara smiled. She enjoyed any compliment but especially if it was coming from him. She knew her cheeks were probably red despite the cold blast from the fridge as she put the bottle away. "Did you come here just to flatter me?"

"Maybe," he answered cryptically as he took another sip. "How's business going today?"

What was he up to? Tara hadn't been sure if she would hear from him right away. Guys always seemed to believe they had to maintain their distance to keep a woman thinking about them, but she doubted Corey was the kind to play games. But then, why not say anything to her about last night? Was he waiting for her to be the first one to bring it up? "Pretty good, actually. Everyone's really getting into the holiday season and ordering all of our specials, so I know I did a good job coming up with them."

"Of course you did." Corey turned as the door

opened once again. He watched the newcomer walk in until she joined her friends at a table. Even once she was seated, he kept his body cocked on his barstool so he could easily see the door. "You're great at what you do."

"And how would you know?" she challenged playfully. "This is the first time you've been here beyond just stopping by for a few minutes."

Corey turned fully toward her again, and Tara could feel that magnetism between them as he studied her lips. "Who says I'm talking about the winery?"

"So you *did* come here to flatter me."

"If that's what you want to call it. Can't a guy stop in to visit his prom date?" He lifted his glass again but didn't bring it to his lips.

"I suppose he can." Tara refilled the supply of napkins, wondering why she was picking up on some tension between them again. He'd come to find her and was the first to bring up their night together. Corey had apologized twice for his past behavior, and Tara had decided to forgive him. So why did she feel like he was so uneasy? If he'd decided he'd made a mistake and didn't want to see her again, then he wouldn't be there. She shouldn't have anything to worry about.

Corey swirled the wine in his glass for a moment. "You looked beautiful last night, by the way."

"Thank you." He'd already told her, but she didn't mind hearing it again. "You looked pretty dapper yourself."

"There's nothing more flattering than a tux. I thought about just keeping it and wearing it everywhere I went, but that might ruin some of the appeal. It's kind of restricting in the gym, so I took it back to the rental place." Corey rolled his shoulders to demonstrate and then turned back toward the customers, scanning the room.

What the hell was he looking for? Most of the diners were making their way out by now, and those who hadn't left were being given their checks. There wasn't much to see. Tara grabbed a knife and began slicing oranges so they'd be ready for the next batch of holiday wine punch, which was proving to be popular. The citrusy scent invaded her nostrils but couldn't distract her completely. Corey seemed like he was waiting for something to happen.

Of course, she had to admit she was a bit on edge herself. Tara was a detail-oriented person, which meant different things in different parts of her life. She had a perfectly organized sock drawer and a routine for cleaning her home. She didn't slack off at work, leaving a task for tomorrow when it could be done right now. And she consistently felt the urge to uncover a situation's details to ensure she understood it completely. Corey had apologized for his past actions but never told her much about that time. Things were still new between them, so it was reasonable for him not to have opened up about it yet, but she still had to wonder.

This wasn't the time, though. Not when they were in public and not when she could feel that Corey seemed to be holding back. Tara decided to just wait things out. After all, she'd already waited this long. What was a little more time? She checked the refrigerated stock. "I've got to take the empties into the back and grab some new bottles. I'll be back."

"Can I help you?" Corey set down his glass and slid easily off his barstool.

"You don't have to do that," she replied. "Enjoy your wine."

He knocked back the last sip and set his glass down. "Consider it enjoyed."

Tara raised a brow. Was he challenging her? Was he trying to figure out a way into her life, or were they both just trying to navigate the new waters they found themselves in? Maybe she was just over-thinking it. She lifted the bar hatch. "If you're sure."

"I wouldn't offer if I didn't mean it." He glanced out at the dining area one more time before he hefted the box of empty bottles.

Tara brought him through her office. It was a place she'd grown accustomed to since she'd moved to Carlton, almost like a second home, but it felt strange to have him see it. Tara quickly slipped through it into the storage area. "The empties go right there. They can be sanitized and reused. Then I need to grab some new ones."

"What kind?" Corey took the new crate she'd grabbed from the corner out of her hands.

It wasn't like she needed to give him a tutorial on running her business, but if he was so insistent on helping, she might as well. "I have a list posted here of all the ones we keep regularly stocked, so some of each. I'll grab the whites. Or not." The bell out on the bar had just rung.

"Go ahead," Corey urged. "I'll get these and be right out. If I have it wrong, you can dock my pay."

She laughed at his mischievous grin and headed back out to the bar. "If you say so."

A man stood there, his cold, dark eyes locked on

hers as he leaned too far forward over the bar. "Your fucking mate killed my brother."

"My what?" Tara shook her head. Running a winery meant that her rowdiest customers were usually still fairly pleasant. This wasn't the sort of place where people drank until they passed out, and no one started shit. Her most belligerent customers were Karens who thought they ought to have a better table.

"Your mate, lady. He killed my brother. Or are you going to tell me you don't know anything about Theo?" The man straightened a little. His dark hair fell in greasy waves against the back of his neck, and his mouth was a hard slash on his gaunt face. His bright blue eyes pierced into hers, daring her to deny whatever he thought happened.

"Listen, I don't know any Theos." Tara glanced at the dining room, but it was completely empty now. It wasn't a shock to see that the diners had left, but even the staff had gone. Her heart thundered. "I think you've already had enough to drink. I suggest you leave."

"He took someone I loved," the man continued. "It took me a while, but I finally tracked his mangy ass down. I know it was him. I can smell him, and I can smell him on you."

Wow, this guy wasn't drunk. He was just a real wacko. "Okay, I think it's about time I called the police." Tara reached for the landline phone that sat tucked up under the bar. It hardly ever got used, but now seemed like the time.

"Not a good idea." The man's arm shot forward so quickly, she had no time to react before his fingers closed around her wrist. He yanked hard, pulling her against the backside of the bar and lifting her feet off the floor.

Pain and panic bloomed in her body as she tried to keep him from pulling her over the bar. Tara reached for something to hit him with, but her free hand fell uselessly on a wet rag. She whacked the man across the face with a satisfying splat. "Let go of me!"

The office door slammed open, and Corey was there. He barreled around the bar and pushed his hands into the man's chest. "What the hell do you think you're doing?"

The stranger let go of Tara's wrist, sending her falling in a heap to the floor behind the bar. She scrambled back up again in time to see him giving that horrifying grin of his to Corey. "You know what you did, and you know you have to pay for it."

Corey's face was hard. "Silas?"

Silas—assuming that was his name—let out a gruff laugh. "So you do remember? Then you know exactly why I'm here."

Tara sure as hell didn't, and she didn't like any of this. "What's going on?"

If Corey heard her question, he ignored it. His focus was entirely on this man, and his face was harder than she'd ever seen it. He didn't even look like himself. "Let's take this outside."

In a mockingly graceful gesture, Silas waved his hand toward the door. "After you, asshole."

Tara rubbed her sore wrist, trying to make sense of what was happening. "Corey, should I call Landon?" she asked, but they were already gone. Desperation flooded her body. She didn't understand anything, but she had to *do* something. She cast around for something to use as a weapon. The little paring knife she'd used on the oranges would sting, but it wouldn't do much against a man. Snagging two of the wine bottles out of the fridge, Tara jogged outside.

"You had no right to come here," she heard Corey growl from around the corner of the building.

Tara headed in that direction, her feet flying across the asphalt of the parking lot. Corey was built and fit, and he was probably far more capable of handling this weirdo than she was, but Tara knew she couldn't just stand there.

"Didn't I?" Silas responded. "Or have you forgotten?"

Forgotten what? And what was the deal with this guy's brother being killed? There were now only more questions she'd need to ask Corey, but again, they'd have to wait. With her hands firmly on the necks of the bottles, Tara sailed around the corner of the building.

What she saw made even less sense than what had happened inside. Corey was there, but Silas was nowhere in sight. Instead, a massive wolf stood in front of him. Its teeth dripped with saliva, and its hackles rose up in a ridge along its back. Its glowing yellow eyes were threatening as it stalked toward its target.

"Tara, get back!" Corey turned and put his hand out, trying to keep her away.

The wolf took its opportunity and lunged, its heavy body throwing Corey to the ground. Tara screamed as she saw its jaws snap, barely missing Corey's throat.

Without her permission or even her thought, her feet flew forward. She swung her right arm up over her head, the smoothness and weight of the wine bottle familiar in her hand. She'd handled so many of them at this point, it was like an extension of her own arm. Whipping it down fast, she let it smash over the wolf's head, the impact sending a jarring vibration up her arm and into her shoulder. Glass shattered, the glistening pieces sparkling in the parking lot lights as they sprayed out in every direction. Red wine poured down the beast like blood.

But it didn't stop him. The wolf turned to her, growling and gnashing his teeth. Tara backed up, realizing she'd made a mistake. She'd lured the wolf away from Corey, but now it wanted her. She was vaguely aware of Corey getting to his feet in her peripheral vision as she swung her left arm around from the side, smashing the bottle into the side of the wolf's face. Several shards of glass pierced the beast's skin, and this time, blood mixed with the wine before it ran down his thick fur and pooled at his feet.

"Tara! Get out of here!"

Both Tara and the wolf turned back to Corey. "I'm not just going to leave you out here alone!"

His eyes were wild as he waved her away. "I'll be fine. Just get out of here. It's not safe. Go!"

Her next protest died on her lips as Corey's shoulders lurched under his jacket. What happened next made so little sense that she hardly knew how to process it. Dark fur burst from his skin. His palms and fingers widened, and thick claws emerged. A ripple of pain crossed his face as sharp fangs descended, and a chilling sound came from his throat as the very shape of his entire face changed. His shoulders were already broad, but now they became even bigger, as did the rest of him. Corey fell forward onto all fours.

But he was no longer Corey. He was a bear. Dark fur covered his body, save for a paler stripe that streaked down his chest. Her stomach curled around her spine as she took in the animal that now faced off against the wolf.

The scream that emanated from her throat rang through the empty parking lot, but it was quickly muted by the roar of the bear formerly known as Corey. He leaned his weight on his hind legs and lunged forward, slamming his front paws into the wolf. His opponent flew backward, landing on his side and skidding across the hard ground.

He wasn't down for long. The wolf scrambled to his feet before Corey could reach him. He charged as Corey approached, clamping his jaws around the thick skin of Corey's neck. Blood trickled down, mixing with the wine that had already puddled on the asphalt.

Tara was sure she was living out a nightmare, but it was one she couldn't wake up from. She heard the impact as the two beasts struggled back and forth, and every snap of their jaws clipped against her nerves. Bits of fur flew into the air, perfumed with the coppery scent of blood. Tara knew she should leave. She should get her ass back into the building, lock the doors, move into the office where there were no windows, and call the police. The logical plan was all there in her mind, yet she couldn't make her body move to enact it.

A massive roar sent a shiver down her spine. It was Corey, if she could even still call him that now. He stood with the wine pooling around his feet, bracing as the wolf charged at him. At the last moment, he ducked his head and shoved himself forward. The sound of their skulls colliding was enough to make Tara sick to her stomach. The wolf flew backward, falling to the asphalt. This time, he didn't scramble to his feet.

Her breath burned as her chest heaved in and out. Tara stared at the wolf's body, not knowing what to think.

"Tara."

He was a man again. Corey was standing there on two feet, looking at her and saying her name urgently. "Tara, are you all right?"

"Am I all right?" she repeated, panic taking over her completely now. She took in all the blood and wine that covered his body, but there weren't any wounds. It didn't make sense. None of this did. "Are you fucking kidding me? Of course I'm not all right! What the hell did I just see?"

"I'm sorry. I'll explain everything later. He's knocked out, but he probably won't stay that way for long. I've got to take care of this. You get inside." Corey reached out toward her, trying to guide her into the building.

Tara snatched her arm out of his reach. "Don't touch me! Don't... just don't!" She glanced one more time at the wolf and then at Corey, but she couldn't handle it. She went inside, not because he'd told her to but because she didn't know what else to do. Cloud Ridge was the only thing that made sense. Her hands were shaking, and she wasn't even sure she had the energy to push the door open. Somehow, she managed to get inside.

The Christmas decorations and lights were warm and friendly, an odd contrast to the horror she'd just been through. She turned to lock the door, keeping her eyes only on the bolt so she wouldn't have to look outside. Whatever Corey was doing, she didn't want to know. The neck of the second bottle was still in her left hand. She stared at it with disdain before slowly moving to the bar and dropping it in the recycling bin.

What the hell had she just seen?

15

COREY'S FISTS COLLIDED WITH THE PUNCHING BAG, focusing on the impact and how it felt as it moved through his body. He hadn't even bothered to turn on his music, knowing it was just a diversion. He wanted to feel all of it. The way his knuckles scraped against the thick material of the bag. The way he shifted his balance on his feet to change where and how the punches landed. It wasn't enough. He lifted his knees, striking them into the side of the bag, but his rage and pain refused to subside. The more minutes that ticked by since he'd last been in his bear form, the more it grew.

He saw those images again, the same ones that had been haunting him for the past year. There were others, too, other things that he was probably responsible for, but they weren't as bad as this one. The wolf at the bottom of the cliff. The feeling of triumph in his chest. The flashbacks were coming so quickly, he could hardly discern them from reality, and they blinded him with guilt and pain. The only saving grace was that, for the moment, it let him focus on something other than how much he'd hurt Tara tonight.

"Corey."

He didn't turn to look, but he knew it was Tyler. "What?"

The beta kept his distance, knowing that Corey needed it. "He's awake."

Corey rammed his fists into the punching bag several more times before he let his arms hang down at his sides. Sweat dripped from his forehead, and heat expanded under his skin. "And?"

"And I think you need to come in. We're going to have to figure this out. Chris is giving him some time to come around, but he's already been muttering your name." Tyler folded his arms across his chest, waiting for Corey to dare to say no.

Corey knew better, but he didn't want to go. "I don't like anything about this."

"That's understandable, but it has to be dealt with. This guy wanted you. You already saw him once, apparently, and now he's attacked you. I don't think you can pretend it's just clan business and not personal," Tyler replied drily.

Was it easy for him to stand there, so nonchalant, as he challenged Corey to face his past directly? "I also saw him several other times."

"You didn't say anything about that."

"I didn't realize it was him." Corey sent another punch wailing into the side of the bag, making it rattle against the chains that held it in place. "It was just a flash of something from the corner of my eye, and I dismissed it. I thought I was just being paranoid. That's what I was told to do, right? To recognize my problems as a symptom of what I've gone through, not reality? Well, that sure as shit paid off."

"I know it's been difficult for you to sort all of this out, but don't be so hard on yourself. Just come with me so we can see what Silas has to say," Tyler replied.

"Fine." Corey knew he didn't really have a choice. He'd have to face this one way or another, and he'd only make things harder for the clan if he was stubborn. They'd done a lot for him, but once they knew the truth, they'd all change their minds.

Moving down a hallway and into the deepest recesses of the clanhouse, Corey followed Tyler into a small room. One side was separated by bars, creating a jail cell. The lights overhead were stark and white, casting everyone in a bleak light. The cold concrete blocks around them radiated the chill they'd picked up from the ground on the other side.

Silas sat on the hard metal bench bolted to the floor. He looked angry and sullen, but he grinned when he saw Corey walk in. "There he is," he announced. "The prick who should be on *this* side of the bars. I'd prefer to see him rotting in hell, personally, but I'll settle for him living out a long, shitty life in prison."

Corey sneered at him. He'd already been locked up. The clan had kept him contained for most of the time he'd lived under the feral curse, for his own safety and that of others. He'd eventually escaped, and now he wished he never had.

He moved closer to the cell but kept a distance between them. "I remember you."

"Yeah, and I remember you, too. I figured I'd be able to track you down, and it was no problem once I picked up your familiar stench. This whole damn place smells of you bears, you know." Silas leaned forward and spat on the floor.

Images hurtled through Corey's mind. They weren't new, but some of the pieces from between them were starting to come back. Before, he'd watched himself fight with a wolf in a series of still images. Now he was getting bits of action, like watching a movie with a glitchy satellite signal that kept dropping out. Teeth. Claws. Rage.

"That's about enough of that," Chris cut in before Corey could say anything else. "Let's get down to the bottom of all this. Your name is Silas, correct?"

The wolf ran his tongue over his front teeth. "Yep."

"And you'd said you're in the Glenwood pack, no?" Chris stood with his hands on his hips, his face neutral.

"Did I stutter?"

Corey didn't know how Chris could stand it. All he wanted to do was get in there and give Silas the same pummeling he'd just given that punching bag.

Chris nodded, matter of fact, as always. "It seems that you were following Corey. Can you tell me why?"

Letting out a little snort, Silas grinned as he continued to stare at Corey. "I could, but maybe you should ask him."

"I'm asking you," Chris said before Corey could reply, his voice picking up volume. "You're the one who stirred up shit on Thompson territory by attacking an innocent human back at that winery."

"Is that my crime?" Silas asked, tipping his head to the side. "Yanking on some bitch's arm? Well, you let me out of here, and I'll go right to her place to apologize. I'm sure I remember her address. I've already been there a few times."

Corey charged forward, ready to rip the bars aside with his bare hands if he had to. "You lay one finger on her, and I swear I'll—"

"You'll what?" Silas teased as the other men grabbed Corey by the arms and yanked him back. "Throw me off a cliff like you did to my brother? Good luck getting that done. It looks like you're just as trapped as I am."

"You good?" Chris asked, a stern look on his face.

Corey wasn't. He wasn't fucking good at all. But he knew what his Alpha was really asking him. Corey gave a single nod.

"Good. Let's cut the bullshit, Silas. Tell me what you're doing here in Carlton and what your beef is with Corey." He waited, his hands braced on his hips once again.

"You didn't tell them?" Silas asked Corey. "I can't blame you. If they knew what a fucking monster you were, they might think about you differently. Actually, you just might be that same monster."

"Spit it out, motherfucker," Corey growled. His bear was writhing inside him, pissed that Corey wouldn't let it out to finish the job it'd started at the winery. "I don't care anymore."

He did, but it was better to just get it over with.

Silas's glance finally moved to Chris. "Your friend here killed my brother. He and I were in the woods as our wolves, walking along this clifftop path, minding our own damn business. So we'd wandered a little further north than we usually did, so what? That doesn't mean we should expect to find a rabid fucking bear in our path."

Chris shot Corey a look as he opened his mouth to speak.

"I knew he was a shifter," Silas continued. "Not like the other bear shifters I'd met, but a shifter, nonetheless. I figured everything was fine. We would go our way, and he could go his. But the bastard attacked us. He was vicious. We were just trying to get away, but he wouldn't leave us alone. I went around behind him, hoping to distract him when he had my brother pinned down. But then he threw Theo right off the cliff and killed him. I thought going after his mate was fair revenge."

Silence descended in the room. Finally, Chris spoke. "I'll be calling your Alpha to find out what to do with you."

"You're going to continue treating me like a prisoner when the real criminal is standing right there next to you?" Silas asked calmly. "That doesn't sound like a good idea to me, unless you want to start something with our entire pack."

"You let me worry about that," Chris advised.

"I'm done here." Corey turned and left the room. He couldn't listen to any more of it. He wasn't even sure where he'd go, but he had to get the hell out of there.

"Corey."

He kept walking.

"Corey," Tyler repeated more firmly.

They were by the door to the gym, and Corey shoved through it. He knew exercise wouldn't help at this point, but he had to try something. He charged over to the free weights. "What do you want from me now?"

"A lot, I guess." Tyler ran a hand through his short dark hair impatiently. "First, I want to know why you're letting that asshole get to you."

Corey let out a sharp, sarcastic laugh. "As if I have a choice!"

"It seems to me like you do." The burly man watched him critically.

"Not when I'm guilty." Corey set the weight down so quickly that it thumped hard against the floor. "He's right, okay? I killed his brother."

Tyler's brow creased. "You were feral."

"Does that really matter?" Corey challenged. "Feral or not, I took someone's life. And for no reason. God." He thought about picking the weight back up again, but it wouldn't do any good. Nothing was going to help him now.

"Call me crazy, but you're acting like this is news to you, like you didn't know about this until now." Tyler stood there like a brick wall, staring him down.

"Not really." Corey didn't want to talk about it, but now it was coming back to haunt him. "I knew I probably did plenty of terrible things when I was feral. I must have. I would get these little bits and pieces of memories. They weren't enough for me to really be able to string together, but lately, they've been getting stronger."

"Maybe since this wolf has been hanging around?" Tyler suggested.

"Maybe." But Corey didn't want to let the blame fall on anyone but himself. He thought he'd made so much progress over the past year, but in one afternoon, it had all gone out the window. He'd wasted his time and everyone else's, and now there was no telling what the clan might do with him. "It doesn't matter. I can see it all now and know Silas is right. I remember that wolf's body lying at the bottom of the cliff, dead. And as soon as Silas showed up at Cloud Ridge, I recognized him. I knew it was him. I'd heard him and his brother talking to each other before they'd shifted, and that's how I knew his name. It's all true, every bit of it."

Tyler sat down on a nearby weight bench and watched him pace. "Even if you did, that doesn't mean it was a punishable offense. It wasn't like it was something you would've done on purpose."

"I appreciate you implying there's a chance I'm innocent, but don't bother," Corey advised. "You're just wasting your time. Damn! Just when I thought I was on the right track. I'd found my fucking mate and everything."

"Why past tense? It looked like you and Tara were fine when I saw you at the prom. In fact, I over-heard plenty of women sighing over how sweet the two of you looked on the dance floor. Made the rest of us fuckers look bad," Tyler grumbled.

"She's not going to give two shits about a few dances together after tonight," Corey argued.

Someone had left a basketball lying nearby. He swung his foot back and kicked it hard, sending it crashing to the other side of the gym. "She saw what I am, and it scared the shit out of her. Silas was going to kill her to get back at me. Even after I saved her, she couldn't so much as look at me."

"Most humans have a hard time understanding us, at least at first," Tyler began.

"It's just as well that she knows what a monster I truly am," Corey cut him off. His frustration had built up so much that even throwing or hitting things wouldn't make it better. "I can't be with her, not if there's something inside me willing to murder someone in cold blood." He twisted his mouth in a sarcastic smile as he turned to face Tyler, feeling the irony of the situation down to his very soul. "I was just about to tell her, too. I was going to tell her the truth, and she would get the chance to decide for herself. But she needed to hear it before she saw it, and that chance flew out the window."

"Corey, I know what you're going through. It might not be the exact same situation," he added quickly, "but it was similar. I found myself in a place where I didn't think I could ever get past my rage and sorrow. My bear was completely out of control. It was Liz—and only Liz—who was able to bring me back to myself. I couldn't tell you all the scientific facts behind our mates and why we feel the way we do about them, but I know something incredibly special is happening there. It's not just a person to be with, and it's not about the sex. It's the other half of our souls, the part of us that we need to feel complete."

"You're not exactly making my loss any easier," Corey reminded him. Sorrow swept over his heart as he thought about Tara. He'd been so close, but now he was further away than ever. He could still see the way she'd looked at him, complete terror on her face.

Tyler let out a frustrated sigh. "What I'm trying to say is that you shouldn't give up on her. It might take her a while, but she'll come around. And then she might be exactly what you need to feel better."

"I don't know about that." He did know, actually. He knew there was no way it could happen.

"The other thing you need to remember is that you aren't feral anymore. The curse was lifted, so you never will be again. Whatever may or may not have happened back then, that's not you. We wouldn't be sitting here talking like this if it was." Tyler stood up and sighed yet again, like an impatient father. "You let me know if you need anything."

Corey didn't respond. What could he possibly need except a chance to redo everything in his life? He'd busted his ass trying to return to some sense of normalcy, and then he'd tried so hard to win Tara over.

He'd failed miserably at both.

16

THE POUNDING ON THE FRONT DOOR HAMMERED inside her chest with her heartbeat. Tara swallowed and slowly stood up, not entirely sure she wouldn't pass out. She raised herself until she could peek over the bar's edge.

"Tara!" her sister screamed from outside, pounding her palm into the door again. "I came as quickly as I could, but I don't have my key on me!"

Bolting around the bar and feeling incredibly exposed, Tara raced to the door. She unlocked it just long enough for Tricia to squeeze inside before she slammed and locked it again. "Thank god you're here. I—I—I don't even know how to explain what I've seen tonight."

"Calm down. Everything is okay. First things first,

do you want me to call Duke? He's on duty, so he could be here in just a few minutes." Tricia put her hands on Tara's upper arms and looked her in the eye, willing her to be all right.

"Yes. No. I don't fucking know! This isn't something the police can handle, and I don't want to get anyone involved who doesn't have to be because it's dangerous. It's crazy. Maybe *I'm* crazy." That thought had been on a regular rotation since all this had happened.

"I'm sure you're not." Tricia leaned forward and sniffed. "Have you been drinking?"

"Not a drop. It's just all over me because I... well, I guess I'll start from the beginning. If I can figure out where that is." Her fingers shook as she brushed her hair out of her face.

Tricia guided her to one of the tables. "Let's sit down."

"Not out here. In the office. Where we can lock the door, and there aren't any windows." She grabbed Tricia's sleeve and dragged her into the back, but once she reached the office, she couldn't sit down. She paced the room, using the motion to make her brain work. "Okay, let's see. I've been trying to get this all straight in my head, but I still don't think it will make sense. I was here at work.

Corey came in. We had just been at the prom last night, and then he came back to my place afterward, so I thought it was about that."

"Oh my god, did you guys finally sleep together?" Tricia interrupted.

"Yes, but that's not the point. Corey came in and we chatted, but he kept watching the door." She did her best to make a coherent story of seeing her boyfriend change into a bear, then get attacked by a wolf-man, but she knew it was impossible. It would never make sense. "I know that sounded insane, and you're probably going to put me in the nuthouse, but I swear I saw it all happen."

Tricia sat in one of the desk chairs. She leaned forward with her elbows on her knees. "First of all, you're not crazy. I believe you."

"You do?" The relief made Tara want to cry. "I'm glad to hear that because I don't think I could go on otherwise."

"I do. Now, can I get you a glass of wine?" Tricia started to stand up.

Tara stopped her. "No. I want to be completely clearheaded while we talk about this. We've got to figure out what to do and who to call, if we can call anyone. I don't know how many of them there are. We might have to leave town."

"A glass of wine might really go a long way," Tricia insisted. "Just one?"

"No!" Tara felt irritation creeping in on the backside of her fear. "I just want to know what to do. I thought I was just about to figure out my whole life, and then this shitshow happened. I don't know why you're so calm."

Tricia steepled her fingers together. "Because I know it's all real. I've seen them, too."

"What?" Tara's shoulders drooped, and she fumbled for one of the other chairs. "You have?"

Her sister swallowed and looked off to the side. "Yes, but it's more complicated than that. Corey may be a shifter, but so are plenty of other people in Carlton. Including Duke and his kids."

"This isn't funny," Tara said with a scowl.

"No," Tricia agreed. "It's completely real. I'll try to sum it up, but it won't be easy. You see, there are a whole bunch of bear shifters in Carlton. They sort of have these family groups called clans. Some of them are actually related, and others are just accepted in. Duke, Landon, and Corey are part of the Thompson clan. It lets them stick together and protect each other."

Tara shook her head, unable to take this in. "That can't be right. This can't be a thing that just happens right under our noses and no one knows about it. They protect each other? From what?"

"Well, there's another clan called the Johnstons around here. They have a beef with the Thompsons that goes way back. I won't go into the details right now, but the two groups are at odds all the time. Duke tries to keep the peace as best he can, but it's not always easy." Tricia reached for her sister.

The room was swinging back and forth, but Tara realized it was because she was shaking her head. "The Johnstons are the ones who tried to take your farm. The ones who trashed it."

"They did more than trash it, and it was the Thompsons who came and helped put it all back together," Tricia explained. "It's just what they do for each other."

"Wait." Tara paused, pinching the bridge of her nose. "Johnston, as in Aunt Fiona and Uncle Dick Johnston?"

Tricia nodded. "Yup. We Fitzpatrick women must be shifter magnets. Turns out Uncle Dick was a bear shifter, too, although he wasn't the best example of one."

Her stomach was rolling. She thought she'd find comfort in her sister's company, but it turned out she was wrong. It was bad enough for Corey to deceive her like this, but her own twin? No betrayal went deeper than that. She felt the wound like a cut across her heart. "I don't get it. You knew about all of this. You *live* in the midst of it, and you didn't tell me?"

"I couldn't," Tricia replied quickly. "It wasn't my secret to tell. Most of the time, it doesn't even matter, because they're living their lives like regular people. But just imagine what would happen if that information got out, if everyone who knew what they really were told everyone else. It could be devastating for them."

"I don't even know if I'm supposed to care," Tara exclaimed, feeling all the frustration, hope, and worry exploding within her at once. "I never knew what happened to Corey, and then he shows up out of the blue. And what, he's a fucking bear? He just snaps his fingers and turns into something else?"

Tricia rolled her shoulders. "Well, they don't snap their fingers."

"That's not the point!" Tara wanted to throw something, but as she looked around the room, she saw how perfectly placed everything was. The collection of framed photos on the wall, arranged just so. The neatly organized desk with its color-coded calendar. The filing cabinet where she could find anything she needed in a flash. She'd worked so hard to make her life as perfect as possible, wanting to keep it all nice and tidy, and now it was just falling apart.

"I've been living a lie," she stated, thinking not only of her habits, but her years-long obsession with Corey. "And even though I feel like a complete idiot for not seeing it before, I can only work on fixing it now. I may be pissed at you, but I'm *never* going near Corey again."

Tricia reached out to her. "Don't say that. He can't help what he is."

"Don't you remember what the other guy said? Corey murdered his brother! And I saw him out there in the parking lot, all fangs, claws, and animalistic rage." Her lungs and throat still burned from her screaming.

"Tara, listen..."

"Why should I? You already didn't tell me that I was dating a fucking man-bear. Aside from that, I can't imagine anything that would make me feel better about this." Tara buried her face in her hands, pressing her palms against her eyes until she saw colors streaking across her vision.

"Just listen," Tricia insisted, more harshly this time. "It doesn't feel like my place to explain this next part, but I think I have to. Corey was living under a curse."

"Right. Because being a shifter is a curse, too?"

"No. It might feel like it at times, but no. It's how they're born, just as you and I were born as boring old humans. But Corey and Landon's family was cursed by a witch a long time ago. It meant that the firstborn of every generation would remain stuck as a bear as soon as they shifted for the first time, losing its human freedoms. Not only that, they would go feral. I don't know what Corey may have done in those years before the curse was broken, but he was essentially living as a wild animal. You can't blame him for it."

"Okay, so the cherry on top of my shifter shit sundae is that it's supposed to be perfectly fine that he murdered someone. Great. Fantastic. So helpful." Tara shoved herself out of her chair once again, wondering how she would ever deal with this. She couldn't. It was as simple as that.

"I know it's hard to understand, and you're going to need some time. You can be pissed at me all you want, as long as you know I'm still here for you." Tricia got up and pulled Tara into her arms.

She resisted at first, not wanting to give Tricia even the slightest hint that she could forgive her for what she'd done. But the truth was she needed her sister. None of the other truths made any sense, but at least that one did. She laid her head on Tricia's shoulder and sobbed. "I don't know what I'm going to do."

Tricia's hands rubbed slowly up and down Tara's back. "You don't have to do anything right now. Knowing about Corey doesn't actually change anything. He's always been a shifter, and he's been working hard to deal with his past. It's just that you're aware of it now. That doesn't mean you have to make any big decisions this second, not when you're still caught up in your emotions."

"I'm not so sure." Tara closed her eyes and thought about the winery, her house, and all the new friends she'd made there in Carlton. It'd been wonderful on so many levels, but could she still go on there? How would it feel to live in a small town and risk running into Corey again? And what about everyone else? She wouldn't even be able to go to the gas station without wondering if the man behind the counter could turn into a snarling beast.

Her sister claimed she didn't have to make any decisions at the moment, but that wasn't how her brain worked. She was instantly weighing different options. She could sell the winery outright, or she could hire someone to manage it for her while she moved off somewhere else. Her house would have to either be sold or rented, which might be difficult this time of year. She might have enough savings to head off to the East Coast for a while and get as far away from this as possible, but she'd still have to deal with what she'd left behind.

And what she was leaving behind, finally, was Corey. Tara had carried him in her heart for over half of her life, always secretly wondering what might have been. There should have been some relief in knowing that what-might've-been was now a never-could-be, but there wasn't.

It only made her hurt all the more.

17

A KNOCK SOUNDED AT COREY'S DOOR, AND IT OPENED a moment later. "He's here."

"Great." Corey looked in the mirror. Was his the face of a killer? He didn't want to find out, but he was about to.

"Are you holding up okay?" Landon asked.

"I think you already know the answer to that." Corey ran a comb through his hair, but it often preferred to do its own thing. Perhaps that was one part of him that was still wild. What about the rest of him? What was he capable of?

"Listen, I know this is going to be hard. It's not fair that you should have to sit down and discuss all of this—"

"More like relive it," Corey interrupted. "Sorry.

It's just that this is more than unfair. I don't even mean on Chris's part. I mean fate or the universe or whatever you want to call it. I was already cursed from the day I was born. I couldn't avoid it, even though I'd tried. And you might say I was lucky enough for that curse to be broken, but am I? If I still have to live with the knowledge of whatever I did while under that spell? And if my mate doesn't want anything to do with me?"

Landon sat down on the corner of the bed. "Have you talked to her yet?"

"Yeah, right. I come waltzing back into her life after twenty-six years, and then she finds out I'm a killer bear. And of course she had to find out the hard way. I don't think there's any point." That was how everything in his life felt right now. What was the point in any of it if it was just going to get screwed up again? Why had he tried so hard?

Landon scratched his jawline. "I get it. Maybe you just need to concentrate on getting through this meeting."

"Don't you mean sentencing?" Corey plucked impatiently at the fabric of his button-down shirt. He'd tried to look presentable, knowing Chris would want to make a good impression, but it all felt so fake. He was just pretending.

"No, I don't. Chris hasn't thrown you in a cell yet, so you need to give him some credit and time. But speaking of time, we're out of it. We need to go." Landon got up and went to the door.

As the two brothers walked down the hallway, Corey didn't know how Landon could possibly see a positive outcome. He kept insisting that Corey be patient and see what happens. He might only be doing it in an attempt to keep Corey's hope up. That was just as fake as this button-down shirt, but Corey knew he'd do the same if he thought it might help. "Thanks for being here with me today."

"I wouldn't be anywhere else."

Downstairs, they turned into the meeting room. It was typically arranged to hold the most people possible. The majority of their clan members came to their meetings regularly, and Corey was used to seeing this space packed. Instead, a singular table had been set up in the middle of the room. Chris was already seated at the head of it, with Tyler to his right. At the other end sat a man that Corey hadn't seen before, but he understood who it was right away.

"Corey, Landon, this is Rex, the Alpha of the Glenwood pack." Chris stood to make the polite introductions. "Please, come have a seat."

"Is Silas not going to be part of this meeting?" Corey asked as he took his place.

"I requested that he not be here for this," Rex replied. He was a burly guy whose limbs didn't seem to quite fit underneath the table, and he carried that same wild strength Corey knew lived in all shifters. His blue eyes burned sharply into Corey's. "I have things to say that he wouldn't like to hear."

"I hope they can help bring the details of this incident to light," Chris replied diplomatically.

"I'm sure." Rex folded his fingers on the table and looked at Chris and Tyler. "If you don't mind, I'd like to start with what Silas told you."

Corey steeled his jaw. He may not be on trial, but he might as well be. It didn't matter anyway because he was guilty. He had the only evidence he needed right there in his mind, and he couldn't erase it no matter how hard he tried. Silas's accusations and those damning images meant he deserved to be locked up, just as he'd been for most of his adulthood.

"Fair enough." Chris cleared his throat. "I should go further back by saying that Silas came up to our town and has been seen by quite a few citizens as his wolf. That in itself isn't an issue, exactly, but he did attack a human woman who's close to Corey. He said that was how he planned to get revenge against Corey, who he claims killed his brother, Theo. He said Corey attacked the two of them in the woods and that Theo was subsequently thrown off a cliff to his death."

Corey's muscles were tight and drawn, his bear restless inside him. He wished the damn beast would just go away because it was evident he couldn't do anything to control it or the situation around him.

"Was the human woman injured?" Rex asked quietly.

Landon shook his head. "She's shaken, of course, but she's safely at home."

Landon knew Tricia had already gone to speak with Tara through Duke. He'd gotten a boiled-down summary of that conversation from Duke, and what Landon had presented to Corey was even more so. Tara was fine, or at least as fine as she could be. Corey knew the betrayal and fear she felt because he'd seen it in her eyes as he'd tried to get her to go back into the winery. He would've done things differently if he hadn't needed to get Silas into custody. He would've stayed with her and tried to explain things. But the way she'd spoken to him had told him it wouldn't make a difference. Tara was lost to him.

"That's good to hear," Rex said with a nod. "Our pack keeps to ourselves, and we don't tend to take humans into the fold. Still, I don't tolerate anyone committing senseless acts of violence on the innocent, human or otherwise."

And what about Corey? He'd committed a senseless act of violence. Despite the images in his head and the rage that easily flooded his body when those memories came, he hadn't been able to find a reason for them. Had he done it just because he could? And would he do it again? It was more than a little uncomfortable to think he couldn't even trust himself.

"Now," Rex continued, sitting forward in his chair, "there's a reason I wanted to come up here and personally discuss this situation. I know it's a bit delicate, for one thing, and I firmly believe that we only benefit from having good relationships with other shifters."

Chris nodded his agreement.

"The other important factor is that I was there."

Corey's vision tunneled, and he could only see the rugged face of the Glenwood Alpha. He hadn't been aware of anyone else being there. What other parts of his memories had been edited out?

Rex ran a hand through his hair. It was cut close

on the sides, the top swept back. "You see, Theo had been causing quite a bit of trouble in our pack. We're very traditional and take care of our own, but he pushed things past my tolerance. He'd been picking fights with other packmates, and I warned him that if he did it again, he'd be banished from the pack. When he and Silas took off, I knew they couldn't be up to any good. In the past, I'd sent other wolves out to keep an eye on them, but this time, I wanted to see things with my own eyes. I trailed them for a while, and I thought they wouldn't do much of anything, but then I saw you." Rex looked directly at Corey.

It was strange to think of anyone seeing him in his feral state, even though he knew people had. Corey waited for the rest of the story, for confirmation that he'd taken Theo's life.

"Theo attacked first," Rex proceeded. "Silas joined in, of course. It wasn't a pleasant scene to watch, but I was high up on a ridgetop. I couldn't physically intervene from that far back, though I tried to communicate with them through our telepathic link. Even my Alpha command didn't get through to them; they were too caught up in the fight. Theo was determined to win and was so focused on the fight that he didn't watch his footing.

It only took one slip of his back paw, and he was over the edge."

"That's very pertinent, indeed," Chris said. He nodded toward Corey. "I know it clears up things for us."

The discussion continued, but Corey didn't hear any of it. He found himself flipping through those echoes of the past, trying to line them up with what Rex had just told them. It was too violent. He was too angry. It couldn't have just been an accident.

"And what about the fact that I was feral?" Corey challenged, interrupting the other men.

Rex gave him that cool regard he seemed to have, one that suggested he'd seen a lot but wasn't bothered by much of it. "Your Alpha explained your situation to me. It's a unique one, but the Glenwoods understand what can happen when one turns feral. What I saw wasn't anything unusual on your part. It was a wild animal protecting itself, doing what it needed to do. It was either them or you, and I know Theo. He wouldn't have stopped for anything, not until he felt he'd won."

"I'd say that takes care of almost everything," Chris concluded. "I assume you'll want to take Silas with you and handle his indiscretions back in Eugene?"

"That would be ideal. I have a few guards with me, but I chose not to bring them to your clanhouse. If you don't mind, I'll get them and come back for Silas. I'm sure he's going to be a handful." One corner of Rex's mouth lifted in amusement.

"Not a problem." Chris stood and came around the table to shake Rex's hand. "I appreciate all that you've done. If you're available, I'd like to extend an invitation to our clan's Christmas party next week."

Rex shook his head. "That's kind of you, but I think I'll pass. Christmas parties aren't really my thing."

"I understand," Chris replied. "If you change your mind, we'd love to have you."

Everyone else was getting up and preparing to leave, but Corey wasn't sure he could move at all. His body felt stiff and cold, and he was tired all the way down to his soul. Even his bear had retreated for the moment, calm and quiet within him as he took in this information.

"Let's get out of here," Landon suggested.

Chris, Tyler, and Rex were still talking when the brothers left the room, just in time to hear Rex say, "You know, I just might accept that invitation after all."

It was all warm and friendly between them now, but what about Corey?

"Are you hitting the gym, the whiskey bottle, or the pillow?" Landon asked as he clapped his brother on the shoulder.

"I don't even know where to start," Corey admitted as they slowly made their way up the stairs. "I've had bits and pieces of those memories, and I'd always thought there was a chance that something terrible had happened. I know now that something did."

"But you also know you're innocent," Landon pointed out. He turned into the kitchen and went to the liquor cabinet, pulling out a bottle of whiskey and pouring them each a couple of fingers in a glass. "I think that's reason to celebrate."

"In a way." Corey couldn't completely deny his relief at knowing what had happened. He'd been far too hard on himself, convinced he was in the wrong. "I would've taken no less than an Alpha who'd witnessed it with his own eyes for me to believe it."

"I know it's going to take some time to wrap your head around this, but that's what your journey has been all about over the past year. It's about time, and healing, and figuring out where your future is going." Landon went to the fridge and pulled out two Cokes to serve as chasers.

Corey accepted his, concentrating on how the cold metal felt in his hand, letting it ground him. "Doesn't seem like I have much of a future besides mooching off the clan."

Landon gave him a look. "Rehabbing isn't mooching, for one thing. You already know that. You'll be starting with the logging company soon enough, anyway. And there's always Tara."

"Is there?" Corey challenged. "I can't pretend I didn't see the look on her face and hear the disgust in her voice. She knows what I am."

"Sort of," Landon amended. "She saw something she didn't expect and probably doesn't know what to think of it. You need to go talk to her."

"I might." He could imagine himself going to her, explaining it all. First, he would tell her he wasn't a murderer, as Silas claimed. That knowledge was enough to change things for him, but would it be enough for her? Corey held an image of her in his mind, listening and understanding, but it faded away quickly.

His brother smiled. "Come on. You were always the peacekeeper. You were the one who wanted everyone to work things out without throwing fists or claws. You've always been the one who made things right, Corey."

Made things right. The phrase echoed in Corey's mind. He'd wanted to make things right for Tara for a long time. He'd already worried it would be too late, even before Silas came around. There had been so many years between them. Was there any chance that he could still do it?

18

TARA PEELED HERSELF OFF THE COUCH. SHE'D BEEN watching holiday classics for a while now, although she couldn't say how long. The winery was shut down for the day because she couldn't bear to go back there when she knew what had happened, and she'd just barely managed to pull on a pair of sweats and a baggy hoodie.

She stretched, feeling how much her joints ached just from one day of sitting around. It should've made her want to get out and do something, but she only wanted to fall right back down on the couch and pull a blanket over her head.

With a deep sigh, she went to the kitchen for a glass of water. A few boxes of pots and pans still needed to be unpacked, the specialty items she only needed for specific recipes. Tara opened the door where her cake pans would go. She stared into the emptiness there and shut the door again.

She stepped into the next room. Her home office would be the ideal space for sitting at a desk and working on reports from the winery or curling up in a comfy chair with a good book. The wide window that looked out over the backyard and the built-in bookshelves were some of the many things that had sold her on this home. All she needed to do was get her books arranged on the shelves and sort her office supplies in the desk. But Tara didn't feel like doing any of it.

Anything that got her more settled into this place felt wrong when she knew there was a good chance she might leave. Tara had exhausted herself with all the possibilities the day before, and now she was stuck in a place of not knowing what her next move should be. That hadn't ever been the way she oper-ated. Tara was a planner and a thinker. She saw several steps ahead in life and had contingency plans ready to go in case things went sideways. Not now.

Checking her phone, she saw several missed calls from Tricia. Tara dismissed them and put her phone on the coffee table. She'd deal with that later.

She'd deal with all of it later, although she had no idea how.

It was getting dark, and the Christmas cards lined up on the mantel reminded her she hadn't checked the mail yet that day. At least she could manage that. A surprise bill or Christmas card might give her a minute or two of distraction from the miserable mindset she'd found herself in.

The evening air was sharply cold as it whisked in through her sweats. Tara stuffed her hands in her hoodie pocket, accepting the discomfort of the cold. The tall trees lining either side of the driveway made it eerily dark, with just a streak of orange still lingering on the horizon to remind her that the sun had been around that day, whether she'd seen it or not. Tara moved slowly, putting one foot in front of the other, going forward in the only small way she knew how.

A shadow detached itself from the trees. Her heart thundered as she saw it move toward her, large and dark. Her feet stopped, and her muscles tensed. Should she run back to the house? Would she even make it?

It took several steps toward her, and Tara knew she was done for. She couldn't outrun a wild creature, and it had seen her. It moved closer, and when it reached the edge of the gravel, she could see with certainty that it was a bear. The chilly evening was nothing against the heat of her blood in her veins.

For reasons she couldn't explain, her eyes drifted down to its chest. A streak of pale fur resided there, one she'd seen before. Her fear morphed quickly into anger, and she shoved her hands deeper into her hoodie pocket as she swiveled back in the direction she'd been walking. "Go away. I don't want to talk to you."

She took several steps, hating the feeling of having him behind her like that. He didn't retreat back into the woods as she'd asked. Tara could feel his gaze on her. "I just learned that everything I thought I knew, and everything I thought I ever wanted, was a big lie. It's a lot to digest, and I just want to be alone."

The bear hung back, but as she continued toward the mailbox, she could hear his steps behind her. They sounded nothing like human ones, not matching her sneakers crunching against the gravel at all, yet he still felt like Corey. That just pissed her off even more. How could he do this to her? How could he taunt her with the truth of what he was?

Tricia had claimed that knowing what he was didn't change anything. In this sense, she supposed her sister was right. But it still did change things. A lot of things.

Tara realized that Corey had caught up with her. He was still keeping his distance, but there was no chance of ignoring him now. As if she could in the first place. Though he looked like any bear she might see in the wild or at a zoo, Tara knew he wasn't there to hurt her. At least not physically. "Maybe I should've forgotten about you years ago, but I always carried this hope that I might run into you again. There'd be some perfectly reasonable explanation, we'd laugh about it, and everything would be okay." She kicked a rock and watched it skip down the driveway.

The footsteps behind her had stopped. Tara turned around to find that Corey was changing back into a human. She'd already witnessed what it was like when he shifted into a bear, but seeing it the other way around was just as disturbing. His body twisted and writhed, and she saw the deep lines that formed next to his eyes as he squeezed them shut against whatever torment was going on within him. Soon enough, he was back to being the same Corey she'd come to know once again, but was he really?

"I never meant to hurt you," he said softly, his eyes pleading. They were tired, and she thought it wasn't just from changing forms. Tara saw the same emotional exhaustion within him that she felt.

She turned away from him and resumed her walk toward the mailbox. "So you've said."

He kept pace with her easily. "I wasn't honest about what happened, but it wasn't easy. I was cursed, Tara."

"I've heard something about that, but I'm not going to pretend I understand." That streak of orange on the horizon was now only the barest twinge of pink, and it felt like they were the only two people left on this lonely planet.

"My family was cursed by a local witch a few generations ago when my grandfather broke her heart. I knew it would affect me, being the firstborn son of my generation. It wouldn't kick in unless I shifted into my bear, and I managed to avoid it for twenty years. But then I had to protect my brother, and I couldn't help it. I knew I needed that side of me to keep Landon safe, and then I was stuck that way for decades. Thankfully, Landon was able to get the curse lifted from our family line before it affected his baby." His voice was as soft and deep as the twilight.

"I hope you know that your explanation doesn't

necessarily make things any easier to take in," Tara noted. "I mean, shifters? A curse? It's crazy."

"I know," he admitted. "It's something I've lived with my entire life, but I can see how it would be totally different for you. That was the problem I had even back then. I couldn't figure out how to tell you the truth about me. I was only twenty and hadn't been faced with telling anyone yet. It's not the kind of thing we often do; sometimes, we don't at all. I had to work out not only how to tell you I'm a shifter but also about the curse over my family and me. Because it's all together in one package. But then I shifted to protect Landon, and there was no chance after that. I was trapped in my bear and went feral, just as the curse had intended."

Finally, she'd reached the end of the driveway. Tara had loved having such a long drive up to her house, almost like her own private road, but now she wasn't sure about it or anything else. She flicked the small metal door open and pulled out a pile of Christmas cards and catalogs. She skimmed over the return addresses without her brain registering who they were actually from. "I don't know what to say, Corey. This is a lot."

"I know." He put his hands in his jean pockets, waiting for her to head back toward the house before he came along with her. "I also know you heard that wolf shifter Silas accuse me of murdering his brother."

"I did." It was no wonder she couldn't take it all in. It was more than could be asked of anyone.

"For what it's worth, he was wrong. I doubted myself because much of the time I was feral isn't very clear. I get glimpses every now and then, ones I'd rather not have to deal with, but they're there. I knew I'd fought his brother, and his accusation had convinced me for a while. But there was a witness, and I now know the truth. I'm not a murderer, and none of that happened the way Silas claimed it did."

She could still feel that gaze on her, as solidly as if he were touching her. "I'm sure you want me to say that's good. And it is, but it doesn't really change things for me."

His shoulders slumped. "I didn't think it would. But I still had to tell you."

Tara frowned as she realized something. She paused, the pile of mail firmly under her arm. For the first time since she'd seen who he was, she turned fully toward him. "Hold on. You said you were trying to figure out how to tell me. Back then, I mean, when we first met."

She still saw that hope and hurt in his eyes. "Of

course I was. I just wasn't prepared for it. I don't think I was prepared for anything, not when it came to you."

A sad smile crossed her face. "I wish I'd known."

"I know." He put his hands lightly on her arms and rubbed his thumbs against her sweatshirt. "I wish I'd been able to tell you. I don't know if it makes any difference now, but I hope it can."

Tara blinked. For a moment there, she thought she might easily fall into accepting it all. She'd already done that when he'd apologized before and when he'd given her excuses about why he'd disappeared. She tore her gaze away from him and looked at her house. The Christmas lights were on a timer, and it looked like something right off the front of a card. Tara had always looked at those kinds of images and thought the people behind those windows could only be happy, but now she wondered.

"Corey, you're asking a lot of me. I mean, in the last twenty-four hours, I've seen my high school crush turn into a bear and then back again. Then there's the fact that this bear was cursed and feral for over two decades. I discovered that there are all kinds of shifters and that they're all around me, even though I never had a clue. Let's add in the fact that my twin sister—the person I trust the most in the world—knew all about this and didn't tell me. Oh, and that she's with a bear-man, too, and raising his cubs. I just... I can't just say, 'Hey, that's okay. At least I know now,' and move on."

"I know." His hands dropped to his sides, and even though he hadn't stepped back, she felt the distance between them widen.

"It does answer a few questions, I guess," Tara admitted. Putting some of the pieces into place was helping it make more sense, although it still wasn't easy. "Now I know why you haven't watched any Christmas movies since the nineties and didn't know half of the songs they played at the prom. It explains why you're not addicted to social media like the rest of us and why you still have a friggin' boombox and CDs." She pressed her hands against her forehead, wishing she could rub out the pain starting to form there.

"All I can say is that I'm sorry," Corey said, his voice so soft that it was barely above a whisper. "I wish I could go back and change all of it."

"I'm sure." She wished the same, but this was the reality that they had to live with now. "I need some time to think, though. I need to sort all of this out in my head. I know you want me to just throw my arms around you and say all is forgiven, but I can't do that."

"I know. I wouldn't expect you to." Corey did take a step back now and put his hands back in his pockets.

Tara opened her mouth, feeling like she should say something, but she didn't know what. She didn't know anything other than the fact it was all incredibly confusing. Clutching the mail tightly, she quickly walked the rest of the distance to the house and up the steps. When she closed the door behind her, she knew that Corey was still out there. She could sense him as though she were looking straight at him. Tossing the mail on the side table, she curled back up on the couch, wondering if her life would ever be the same again.

19

"THAT'S ABOUT IT," CARMEN SAID AS SHE FINISHED balancing the cash register and zipped up the bank deposit bag. "Merry Christmas Eve."

"Merry Christmas Eve to you, too. And here. I don't want to forget your gift." Tara ran back into the office.

Cloud Ridge had become the center of her life since she'd moved to Carlton. She'd wanted to do the best job possible, not only to honor her late Aunt Fiona, but because that was just the type of person she was. To her, nothing was worth doing if you weren't going to give it your best effort.

But over the past week, it had become more than that. It was her grounding space, a place that let her draw clear lines in her life, keeping her from flying off into a mindless sea of worry and anxiety. She had work to do there, which meant she was getting up and getting dressed every day, even though some days, she could just lay in bed forever. The winery and its prosperity also told her that even though she'd had one failed marriage and another rocky relationship, she could still be successful.

Grabbing the last of the small red envelopes from her top desk drawer, Tara handed it to Carmen. "Just a little something to let you know how much I appreciate you."

"Well, thank you!" Carmen replied with a grin. She eased it open, and her eyes widened. She looked at Tara and then back at the check in her hand. "Are you sure?"

Tara laughed, a sound that felt strange coming out of her mouth after all she'd gone through. "Of course, I'm sure. It's a Christmas bonus, and you deserve it. I think a lot of you, Carmen. You really help keep this place going."

"Thank you. Thank you so much. I'd better get home. My boyfriend and his family are waiting for me to start our traditional Christmas Eve dinner. He's going to be thrilled. We've been talking about buying a house together, and this will top off what we've saved up for a down payment!" Carmen hugged Tara tightly before she shot off to grab her coat and purse.

On her way out the door, Carmen paused. She turned back to her boss with concern on her face. "Tara, I don't know if you have any plans tonight, but you're more than welcome to join us for dinner if you'd like."

"That's all right. I very much appreciate it, though. You have a Merry Christmas." Tara plastered on a smile until Carmen was out the door and trotting to her car.

Then she let the smile go and took a moment to walk through the dining area. The huge Christmas tree, the gorgeous tables, the evergreen swags. She'd put it all together in the hopes of making the winery feel like home, a place people could gather with their loved ones and truly celebrate. Lots of patrons thought she'd done a good job, considering the business they'd been getting.

Despite her efforts, it didn't make a cozy home for her. Tara knew why Carmen had invited her to dinner. She didn't talk about her personal life at work, but Tara knew it was apparent how distracted and down she'd been. No matter how much she'd thrown herself into her job, that stabbing stillness in her heart could make her stop what she was doing and lose herself in thought.

Starting in the back corner, Tara began putting the chairs up on the tables to give the place a thorough sweep. She didn't really have any place to go that night, but she didn't want to take advantage of the pity that Carmen and her boyfriend's family would show her. Technically, she could go over to Tricia's house. She'd been invited, and she and her sister had managed to have a few conversations that were far less tense. But the thought of being in someone else's picturesque Christmas card was just too heartbreaking.

She moved slowly, knowing she had all the time in the world. Tara could get home as late as she wanted, and no one would mind. No one was waiting for her to unwrap the presents under the tree or sip cider by the fire. Her shoulders ached with a tension that wouldn't leave even when she slept, making her wake up sore and cramped every morning.

A knock sounded on the door.

"We're closed," she called without looking. On any other day, she would've opened the door and offered to sell them a bottle of wine even if the kitchen was shut down but not today. She couldn't handle it.

The knock came again.

"Look, I said we're—" Tara turned around to shoo the would-be customer away, but she stopped when she saw who it was. Corey stood there with two paper bags in his hands.

Tara stood still, frozen, but felt her heart lurch inside her chest. She'd thought about calling him but hadn't been able to make herself do it. Her heart ached every time he crossed her mind, which meant she was suffering constantly. She just didn't know how to fix it.

Slowly, she crossed the room and unlocked the door. "Hi."

"Hi." He held up the bags. "I had Drew over at The Warehouse make up something special for us, if you'd like to have a Christmas Eve dinner with me. I figured you could use it after a long day. I heard you've been keeping pretty long hours here."

"I have," she admitted as she let him in.

The only open table was closest to the fireplace, the one every sweetheart couple tried to request. It was there that Corey deposited the bags and began to unload them. He arranged containers of roasted turkey, garlic mashed potatoes, herbed green beans, and creamed corn. "He said he could do something a little more gourmet, but I thought traditional might be more of what you wanted."

"Traditional is nice. I'll get some plates." As she headed into the kitchen, Tara slowed. Was this really what she was doing? Sitting down and having Christmas Eve dinner with a bear? It was such a strange idea, but every part of her demanded that she do it. She had to give this a chance. She had to see what it all meant.

When she returned, Corey was unpacking fresh, hot, buttermilk biscuits. "I've been worried about you," he said as they sat down.

The fire was low, barely more than the hot embers leftover from crackling along merrily all day. Tara felt its heat, but Corey's concern for her warmed her from the inside. "That's kind of you. I've been a little worried myself, but I've also wondered about you. I... I wasn't sure how you were after the way we left things last week."

Picking up a knife and fork, Corey took a bite of his turkey before he answered. "It's hard to describe, really. I guess I kept hoping you'd show up one day, that you'd be looking for me as much as I've been looking for you. We had no chance of seeing each other for the longest time, but knowing that you're never more than a few miles away from me has been tough."

"I know," she admitted, because it was the truth. Tara hadn't talked to anyone about how she felt, not even Tricia. As far as she was concerned, the subject of Corey simply wasn't up for discussion. Tara hadn't wanted anyone's input but her own because whatever her decision was, it had to be completely genuine.

"Tara." Corey put down his silverware and reached across the table. He took her hand, holding it in both of his own. "I can't ask you to do anything you're uncomfortable with, and I won't. Even if this dinner is too much for you, I'll go. I know how badly I've hurt you, and I don't want to keep doing that. I'm not here to ask you to make any major decisions or to fall into my arms and make all my dreams come true. I'm only here to ask if there's any possible way you could forgive me. You don't even have to forgive me today, but if I know there's a chance you could, it would be the best Christmas miracle I've ever had."

Pain swept through her heart. Tara had taken her time, and even though it didn't seem like enough, she knew she'd made her decision. "Corey, I've waffled back and forth, weighing this against that.

There were pros and cons and all sorts of points in between. I kept looking for some rational ground from which to make my decision because that's how I operate. I like seeing things in black and white, but this whole thing has felt like a big cloud of grey. The one thing I keep coming back to, though," she continued, "the one thing I can't rationalize or even make any sense of is that I'm drawn to you. I have been ever since we met. It's not just physical attraction, although of course that's there. It's something more. Like my heart just isn't complete without yours."

His breathing grew deeper, and he clutched her hand more tightly. She thought she saw the shimmer of a tear in the corner of his eye, but when he blinked, it was gone. "You don't know how happy I am to hear that."

"There's something else, though." She looked down at the table, and though she meant to study the weave of the tablecloth, she saw their hands. Corey had both of his wrapped around hers, but she was clutching his just as tightly. "You asked for my forgiveness. You have it, Corey, because you never really needed it anyway. It wasn't your fault that you left. I know that now. It's not even your fault that you didn't tell me right away, either back then or this time around. How could you? Hell, I don't know that I could if I were in your situation. I only want to know if you can forgive me."

"Forgive *you*?" Corey leaned forward, his brow creased. "For what?"

"For not giving you a chance. For assuming all of the worst things simply because they were out of my realm of understanding. For turning away from you every time you *did* try to tell me. I wasn't being fair, and I'm ashamed of the way I acted toward you." She let out a long breath, realizing just how good it felt to get all of that off her chest. It hadn't been easy, but it was a relief not to have that bottled up inside anymore.

"I don't blame you for that. You said I don't need your forgiveness, and I'll tell you the same. I don't see anything wrong with what you did, Tara. I don't think I ever could. Come here." He rose from the table, lifting her hand and pulling her gently into his embrace.

Tara leaned into him, her cheek on his chest and her arms around him. It was cold outside, but she felt more warmth and comfort in Corey than she'd known for most of her life. Tara felt tears burn her own eyes as she realized just how long she'd been looking for this feeling. She'd found it once before when she was just a girl who thought she knew everything, but she'd never been able to find it again. Until now.

"I hope I didn't sound like a weirdo with all of that talk about feeling like I'm being pulled toward you," she said, inhaling the familiar scent of his cologne.

"You're the one worried about sounding like a weirdo?" His laugh was a low rumble against her ear, and he rubbed his hands slowly up and down her back.

She smiled against his chest. "It's just the strangest thing I've ever felt, and I don't know how else to describe it."

"There's a lot we'll have to discuss about who and what I am, but I guess this means we should talk about one thing in particular right now."

She pulled her head back to look up at him, a little worried. "What is it?"

Corey cradled her cheek in his hand and laid her against his chest once more. "Shifters believe there's one person for them in the world, the person they're destined to be with, the one the universe brings them back to again and again. We can feel it inside us. It's a pull, a demand, a connectedness. It's how we know we've found our one true mate, and I know I've found it in you."

"Oh." Tara thought about that for a minute. It was just as strange as everything else she'd learned recently, but maybe a good kind of strange. "I think I like that."

When she lifted her head this time, he leaned down to press a kiss against her lips. It was warm and sweet and expanded that delectable comfort he'd already brought to her by just being nearby. Tara melted into it, letting her body relax against him. He was solid, all muscle. She was fully aware a bear was inside him, but she didn't fear it. She trusted him.

Corey's hand moved down past her lower back until he cupped her backside, pulling her closer. He inhaled deeply, as though he couldn't get enough of her. His fingers were strong and demanding, needful as they touched her.

A moan issued from her throat as she wrapped her hands around the back of his neck and pulled him closer. She'd missed him so much and let herself get so caught up in the details. It was what she did most of the time, but right now, it didn't matter. She only wanted him. Tara felt the power of her feelings rise within her as she clutched at him, trying to get as close to him as possible.

His tongue parted her lips, its warm, velvety touch sliding against hers. Corey took her face in his hands and kissed her more deeply, and she knew without asking that he wanted her just as badly as she wanted him. Not just physically. It was more than that, so much more.

Tara stripped back his jacket, letting it fall carelessly to the floor. She skimmed her palms over his broad chest and moaned into his mouth as she felt his warmth. As delectable as he felt through his shirt, she knew she wanted more. She found the hem and lifted it.

Corey's fingers easily slipped her buttons free of the fabric that surrounded them, and Tara felt a brief breath of cool air against her skin as he exposed her. His kisses dropped from her lips to her jawline, down her throat further. They were soft and warm against her skin as he unclasped her bra and sucked her nipple into his mouth, caressing it with his tongue.

A jolt of excitement bolted through her body to her core. Tara closed her eyes as she tipped her head back, feeling every stroke of his tongue against her sensitive skin. They'd had each other before, but this time it was different. This time it was slow and deliberate, a reminder that this wasn't merely attraction.

Without looking, she managed to flick aside his belt buckle. The rest of their clothes were easily cast aside as they sank down in front of the fireplace. Tara felt the heat of the embers radiating out, but it was nothing compared to the heat that Corey stirred inside her. She slid her thighs against the outside of his, already quivering with anticipation of what was yet to come.

Corey sank down on top of her and slid inside her entrance. They held each other there for a long moment, reveling in how well they fit together. Tara wrapped her legs around him and kissed the side of his neck, inhaling the scent of his skin. It wasn't just his woodsy cologne, but *him*. She swore she could even smell his need for her, and all of these animalistic feelings had her dragging her teeth against his shoulder.

They moved together as he began to thrust faster and harder. Tara felt herself tightening around his shaft, her body winding up as she took him all in. She loved the way his skin felt against hers, how he grunted softly when she ran her fingers up the back of his neck and through his hair. They were everything together, and she could feel his excitement building even as her own did.

Corey pulled back on his elbows just enough so he could kiss her again, plunging the depths of her mouth and core. That tightness inside her expanded and contracted, rippling through her body and sending waves of heat and light throughout her limbs. She felt his reaction inside her, triggering her own all over again as she moaned into his mouth. Her fingernails dug into his back as she pressed into him, taking and giving, demanding everything of him but wanting to give him the same pleasure.

With one final, desperate shudder, Tara felt her body melt. She let her head rest against the floor as she caught her breath, and the details of the room came back to her. They were right there on the floor of the winery, but she couldn't care less.

He smiled down at her as his thumbs gently whisked her hair out of her face. Corey pressed kisses on her cheeks and forehead, still loving her.

She'd avoided saying it for so long because she thought it could never be, but she knew it to be true. She'd been silly ever to doubt it. "I love you, Corey."

He pressed one long, final kiss to her lips. "I love you, too."

She looked up into his eyes, knowing they'd only

barely scratched the surface. "Now tell me the rest of it."

"That's going to take a long time," he laughed softly.

Tara rolled her shoulders and wrapped her arms around him. "We have all night."

20

"ARE YOU SURE YOU'RE OKAY WITH THIS?" COREY squeezed her hand gently as they walked up from where he'd parked the car.

She worried that she was overdressed in a dark green sheath with long sleeves that flattered her figure and her hair twisted up on the back of her head. Now that they were there, she was hardly thinking about her outfit as she tried to take it all in. Tara's eyes were everywhere, having a hard time deciding where to land. Every angle of the house was outlined in lights, and every tree was wrapped from the trunk to the tip. It let her see just how much was there, even in the dark. "This place is huge," she murmured.

He looked up at the clanhouse and shrugged. "It

is, but like I said, it's not like one person owns it. The whole clan does. With logging and other ventures, there's plenty of money available to go into it. And, I guess you kind of get used to it."

Tara wasn't sure she would. No, that wasn't really true. She was already adjusting to so many things about Corey's life that just yesterday had seemed almost unbelievable. Tons of cars were already parked there, trailing the sides of the long driveway almost down to the road. So many shifters called Carlton their home, and this wasn't even half of them.

Stepping up to the front door, it was opened before Corey could even reach for the knob. Landon stood there with Michelle at his side. "I thought I saw you walking up," he said as he gripped his brother's hand and elbow. He grinned at Tara. "You managed to clean him up pretty well."

"I can't take credit for any of this," Tara admitted, "but he does look handsome in a suit."

"With the prom a few weeks ago, we've probably exceeded our allotment of dressy occasions for a while," Michelle laughed. "They'll be in jeans and sweats until next Christmas."

"Hey, now," Landon protested with a smile.

Michelle shrugged, her dark eyes twinkling at him. "You still look hot in your sweats, honey."

Corey and Tara followed them into the house. From what she'd seen outside the home, Tara knew to expect something nice, but this place was incredible. The large foyer served as a gathering space, but given what she could see through several doorways, there were plenty more rooms where people had gathered. The Christmas decorations looked professionally done, with not an ornament out of place on the massive tree. Thick evergreen garland had been wound with ornaments and lights and draped over the mantel. A wide gold ribbon wrapped around the banister, ending in a huge bow that a little girl was enthusiastically pointing at.

Tara realized she knew exactly who that little girl was and lifted her eyes to see Tricia standing next to her.

"You're right, Mia," Tricia was saying patiently. "Something like that would look very pretty in our house. Maybe we can go out to the after-Christmas sales and find some new decorations."

The girl looked up. "What's an after-Christmas sale?"

Tricia laughed. "You'll find out. You'd better get over there by the tree before things get started." As she straightened, Tricia locked eyes with Tara and held out her arms. "You're here! I knew you said I'd see you tonight, but I thought you meant after all this!"

Tara hugged her sister tight. "I thought I'd make it a little surprise."

"A little?" Tricia's eyes flicked back and forth between Tara and Corey. "It's a freaking huge surprise!"

Corey slipped his hand into Tara's once again. "We managed to work things out."

That was one way to put it, and Tara couldn't wait for them to work things out all over again. She smiled at her sister, feeling the glow of the holidays within her. "I'm sorry I was so secretive over the phone, but I wanted you to find out in person."

"No, that's all right. I'm thrilled. I know all of this hasn't been easy, but I'm always here if you need me." Tricia held both of Tara's hands in her own and looked like she was going to cry.

"Now, don't start any of that," Tara warned gently. "You'll ruin your makeup."

"I know." Tricia flapped her hand at her face. "I'll do my best. Oh, it looks like they're going to start."

"Ladies and gentlemen," said a broad-shouldered man with deep auburn hair. He stood in front of the Christmas tree with a curvy brunette at his side and waited patiently for the crowd to quiet down.

"I told you about our Alpha, Chris. That's him and his mate, Brandy. I'll introduce you to them in a little bit."

Tara nodded, hoping she could keep all the names straight. She already knew quite a few people there and recognized others she'd seen around town. Some faces were new, of course, but she had a feeling she'd end up knowing them all soon enough. After all, Corey seemed quite tied to this clan of his. It sounded like a giant family where everyone supported each other, no matter what. Tara knew that wasn't an easy thing to come by.

"I need all the children to come up here," Chris said. "I see we've already got a few. Yes, you too, Kinsley."

A teenage girl Tara recognized as Shannon's daughter threaded her way toward the Christmas tree, looking embarrassed.

"I think that's everyone. Let's see who the first gift is for." Brandy lifted a shining red package out from under the tree. "Baby Corey."

"Aww!" Michelle stepped up with Corey's nephew in her arms and accepted the gift for him.

"Oliver," Chris read off the next label. "And Mason and Mia, as well."

Duke and Tricia's children stood eagerly nearby, and the twins looked especially excited.

"Is this something they do every year?" Tara asked quietly.

Corey was at her side with his arm draped around her waist. "It's been a tradition for a long time, even back when I was a kid. The Christmas party has always mostly been for the adults, with food and dancing, so they make sure the kids get a little something out of it, too."

"Quincy," Brandy called out. "Robert."

Two small children approached, looking a little apprehensive. Their mother was behind them. Tara thought she was a friend of Shannon's named Rachel, but they hadn't been formally introduced.

A slew of other children came through as their names were called, ranging from infants all the way up to older teens. The adults waited patiently, all smiling and happy as they watched the kids get their gifts. Even the children waited patiently with their wrapped presents in their hands as everything was passed out. Once again, Tara couldn't believe what a delightful little community this was.

"That's everyone!" Brandy announced.

The room became a flurry of wrapping paper, ribbons, and squeals of delight. Even some of the teens risked small smiles while they showed each other what they'd gotten. They all pitched in to help clean up the mess afterward, with no one stopping until everything was done.

"I'm impressed," Tara said when the gift-giving was through, and the party had resumed.

"Why is that?" Corey was looking at her with that soft gaze in his eyes, the one that made Tara feel all the desire and love he had for her as though she were standing right in front of the fireplace.

"It's generous, sweet, and just one of the most wholesome things I've ever seen." She rolled her hand through the air, trying to think of how to explain it.

"What? Did you think we'd all just turn into bears and go catch salmon in a creek for Christmas?" he teased.

"I guess I wouldn't know, would I?" she quipped right back. "There's a lot I still have to learn."

"Oh! You also have a present from Santa. Come here." With his arm still around her waist, he guided her over in front of the Christmas tree.

"You don't have to give it to me here," she whispered, realizing that several pairs of eyes were already watching them.

"I want to," Corey said softly. "You deserve it and so much more."

When they reached the tree, Corey turned her around so that he faced her in front of it. Tara watched him in confusion. She didn't see how he'd had time to find a gift, and he didn't even have a box or a bag. Her cheeks heated as she noticed almost everyone in the room looking at them now.

"Tara." Corey knelt down on one knee.

Tara's mouth fell open. She glanced up to see her sister and Duke standing on the other side of the room. Tricia was hopping up and down and smacking Duke excitedly on his arm. He merely smiled at her. Landon was on the other side of him with a satisfied smile on his face.

"I can never fully explain with words what you mean to me," Corey started, his fingers warm against hers. "You are the woman I've always longed for. I've already had to live so much of my life without you, and I don't ever want to do that again. I want to be with you the way we were always meant to be. Tara, will you marry me?"

From his jacket pocket, he produced an exquisite opal ring with deep sapphires on either side of it.

Tara saw the glittering ring and the way it twinkled in the Christmas lights, but even more so, she saw the love in Corey's eyes. "Yes." She'd overthought so many things over the last few weeks and even the last few years, but there was no deliberating this any longer. Corey was a part of her, and she was willing to accept every part of him. "Absolutely."

His fingers shook as he slipped the ring on, and everyone cheered as he pulled her into his arms and kissed her tenderly. Corey pulled back just a fraction so that their lips grazed as he spoke. "Even with all of this craziness?"

Chris popped the cork on a champagne bottle off to their left. "It's time for a celebration!"

Tara giggled as Brandy handed her the first glass. "Definitely."

The floor cleared and the music cranked up. Couples swayed and laughed, spun and dipped. Tara clung to Corey, never wanting to let him go. "You're incredible, you know that?"

"I've had a lot of help." Corey gave a nod to someone across the room.

When they turned, Tara expected it to be Landon. She knew what a huge part of Corey's life his brother was, which was something she could certainly understand. Instead, she saw a tall, brawny man who looked a little guarded and out of place at this party. "Who's that?"

"That's Rex, the Alpha of the Glenwood pack," Corey explained softly.

"I see." Tara felt like thanking the man herself because she knew what a big difference he'd made, allowing Corey to realize he wasn't the horrible beast he'd feared.

Rex, however, seemed a bit occupied at the moment. An old woman with stooped shoulders and a long gray braid marched up to him. She wore a baggy cardigan with Christmas trees and wreaths appliqued all over it. "You look like you could give me a little bit of Christmas spirit," she remarked as she poked Rex in the chest. "Come on, or are you too chicken?"

The wolf's eyes widened, but he kindly followed her out onto the floor. To Tara's surprise, the old woman more than kept up with him, dancing with all the energy of someone half her age. When the song ended, she winked at her partner. "My name's Lenora, by the way. Look me up if you want to have another good time." She pinched Rex on the ass before he could make his way off the dance floor.

Two hours later, when her feet were sore from dancing and she thought she might never want to drink eggnog again, Tara stood on her porch, unlocking the front door. Corey was at her side, as he'd been all night and as he would be forever.

"What are you smiling about?" he asked as they stepped inside.

The Christmas lights were already on, thanks to the timer, and she basked in their warm glow while it lasted. She'd be taking them down soon enough, but she knew she'd have something much better to keep her warm at night. "I'm happy to be home, for one thing, and even more to know that you'll be here with me."

He pulled her tightly into his arms and pressed his lips against hers. "So you liked your Christmas gift?"

"Mmhmm." Energy and excitement swirled inside her. "I think I'm ready to show you just how much I appreciate it."

"You can, but you have one more gift first." He pulled back and stepped away. "It's in this room, and you have to find it."

Tara raised an eyebrow. "Is it in your pants?"

Corey laughed, a sound she loved just as much as the rest of him. "Maybe later, but that's not the one you're supposed to be looking for right now."

Scanning the room, Tara wondered how she was

ever supposed to find it. There was no big package sitting anywhere obvious. But then her eyes landed on the tree, and she spotted an ornament that she definitely hadn't put there. She gasped as she delicately touched the little clay bear holding a candy cane, the same one they'd seen in the craft booth weeks ago. "You went back and got it."

"I kind of had to," Corey explained. "That was before you knew what I was, but you still picked out a bear. It gave me some hope that things might work out for us."

"Oh, Corey." She melted into his arms, wondering if she'd ever been this happy before. "You're so sweet. This has been the perfect Christmas."

"I'm glad to hear it. I didn't have a whole lot of time to try, but I did my best." He skimmed his hands down her spine and onto her backside.

"You don't even have to try," she told him. "Just being with you and knowing you're thinking of me is enough."

A car door slammed outside, making them both turn. "Was there something else you were planning for this evening?" she asked.

"Nope." Corey crossed to the door and opened it. Frigid air blew in as Tara peeked out, swirling around her knees where they were exposed by the dark velvet. She didn't recognize the car that had pulled up, and the plates looked like rentals. She did, however, recognize the two people who got out. "Josh? Lauren?"

"Merry Christmas, Mom!" Lauren dashed up the stairs and onto the porch first. "Surprise!"

"Well, I'd say." Tara squeezed her tightly, hardly believing she was really there. "I didn't think I was going to see you."

"We changed our plans," Josh explained. He'd paused to grab their bags out of the back, lugging them up and dropping them in the living room before giving Tara a hug of his own.

As thrilled as she was to see them, Tara couldn't help but be concerned. "But your interview? And your job?"

Josh flapped his hand dismissively. "I told them we'd have to wait until after the holiday. If they're not willing to wait, I don't want to work for them anyway."

"And I managed to find someone to cover my shift," Lauren explained. "I didn't think I could, but one of the other girls there isn't celebrating until later in the month when everyone else in her family is available. She offered to help me out."

"That's so sweet. I'm so happy." Her mind started churning as she realized she needed to turn out a perfect Christmas on the spot, and then panic set in. "But your gifts! I already mailed them."

"And we brought them with," Lauren enthused. Her eyes flicked curiously to Corey.

Tara realized she was being a bad hostess. "Oh. These are my children, Josh and Lauren. Kids, this is Corey."

Lauren blinked. "You mean, like, *the* Corey?"

"No way. The Corey Story guy?" Josh asked.

Corey turned to Tara. "I take it that means you've talked about me."

"Maybe a little," she admitted. She turned back to Josh and Lauren. "We happened to find each other again, and, well, we just got engaged tonight." Tara held out her hand.

"What?" Lauren shrieked. "You're kidding! Oh, my god! That's amazing!" She hugged her mother, then Corey, and then her mother again.

Josh had always been much calmer than his sister, but he showed his enthusiasm in his own way with a smile and a handshake for Corey. "Congratulations."

Tara was nearly falling over under Lauren's excitement, and she laughed as she braced herself against Corey to straighten up. "All right! All right!" she laughed. "You two go upstairs and pick your rooms. I'll put some snacks together."

"They seem great," Corey said as he followed Tara into the kitchen. "I take it all of this means they approve?"

Tara smiled and nodded. "Definitely."

They say young love doesn't last, but Tara never quite believed it. She may not have seen Corey for decades, but she'd held him in her heart the entire time. And now, she'd never let him go again.

THE END

Thank you for reading *Bear's Midlife Christmas*!

Follow my next series for more midlife adventures with Rex and the Glenwood wolf pack. Read on for a preview of Marked Over Forty's first book, *Forbidden Midlife Mate.*

REX

"Happy freaking New Year to me," Lori Jensen muttered, poking at the touchscreen of her new fitness tracker. She'd just gotten it, and even though everyone made them sound so easy to use, she hadn't quite figured the thing out yet. At forty-eight, she was experiencing the joys of perimenopause, and her doctor had pushed her to start moving more to ease her symptoms. Exercise wouldn't stop her hot flashes, but she'd hoped it would at least get her energy and mood back on track. She couldn't use the excuse of being a busy mom anymore now that Conner was in college.

"Oh, hell. Jogging is still good for me even if the damn thing doesn't keep track of it." Slamming her car door and making sure she had her keys tucked in her pocket, Lori got started.

Eugene was new to her, and not a city she'd picked for herself. It was... *different*, that was for sure. Everyone seemed to be outside all the time, and she couldn't blame them, with the mild winter weather and all. It felt odd to be outdoors in January without a heavy parka, a hat, and thick gloves, but she had to remind herself she wasn't in Chinook, Montana anymore.

She wasn't the only one out for a jog that day. The wide gravel paths were bustling with people. Parents walked with their small children, who dragged them off to a nearby playground. A bicyclist or two rode by, and Lori picked up her pace. She was tired, but that wasn't going to stop her. She could do this.

"Excuse us!"

Lori bolted to the right as a group of fit young college girls came darting past. While Lori had donned her sweats and a dingy old bra, these girls were slim and lithe in their stylish athletic wear, showing off their perfect shapes in their clingy leggings, form-fitting sports bras, and cropped hoodies. Their ponytails wagged as they passed by, mocking Lori for going so slow.

She snorted to herself, remembering how she, too, had once been young and lithe, thinking she'd remain that way forever. "Enjoy it while it lasts, ladies. Gravity's a bitch."

A loud beep had her looking down at her fitness tracker. It was finally working, or at least she was pretty sure it was. She had no clue what all the numbers and symbols meant, but it was obviously doing something. Good. She was really doing this. Not just the jog, but everything. This was the start of a whole new life for Lori, and she was determined to make the most of it.

Her muscles burned, reminding her that all the years of running the saloon with Chuck hadn't been the same as getting proper exercise every day, even though she'd spent most of her shifts entirely on her feet. Of course, she probably wouldn't have had to bust her ass so much if Chuck had bothered to do his job.

It was supposed to be fifty-fifty when they'd first opened The Wagon Wheel. It had always been Chuck's dream, but he'd never had the money. Lori had just been given a small inheritance from a great-uncle, but the fact that the man she'd loved wanted her to be involved in his business had been sweet and flattering. They'd bought the cheapest old building in Chinook and transformed it from a sad little wreck on the outskirts of town to a hopping saloon everyone clambered to on the weekends. Even the weekdays weren't too dull once Lori had talked Chuck into doing theme nights and serving better food. People were bored in their little town, so they loved the chance to see their friends over a beer while playing darts. They loved it even more when there were holiday parties, charity events, and pool tournaments.

But as hard as she'd worked, nothing was quite good enough for Chuck. Lori thought she'd made him happy, but she knew she was wrong when he ran off with the hostess.

Lori had let her mind completely wander, and with a jolt, she realized she'd gone way further than she'd ever thought she would. She glanced at the tracker on her wrist, wondering if she really had gone over a mile. That would explain why her lungs burned. Lori slowed to a brisk walk. She could feel her heart thumping, but it wasn't setting her device off, so it couldn't have been too bad.

Lori grinned. This really was a whole new start for her. This wasn't the kind of thing she would've done if she'd stayed back in Chinook, listening to all the locals whisper behind their hands about how

Chuck had run off, thinking she didn't hear them. She'd never been happier about moving away because the last thing she wanted was for anyone to think she was doing this just to get back at Chuck. It didn't have a damn thing to do with him, nor did anything else in her life. She was finally *free.*

A black shape fluttered in front of her. Lori turned to follow it, spotting the raven just as it landed in the grass on the other side of the path. It cocked its head to the side, studying her.

"Well, hello." She paused, knowing she couldn't stay still for too long and lose her momentum, but it had so much personality. "You look like you're trying to tell me something."

It opened its thick black beak and let out a jittering call before moving a few steps away from her.

"Oh, it's okay. I'm not trying to hurt you. I've always liked animals. I mean, it's not like I have any pets right now. I just moved here, and my landlord doesn't allow them."

Another cry issued from the raven's throat just before it flew into the air, swooped between a few trees, and settled into a low branch.

"I wish I knew what you were saying." But something inside her knew the bird wanted her to follow it. Lori had always felt animals knew far more than people, and she'd been looking for signs to let her know she was heading in the right direction by moving out to Eugene. Perhaps the raven was telling her just that.

When she reached the base of the tree, the raven swept off for another one.

The trail was getting narrower. Lori realized she hadn't seen any joggers or cyclists for a while, and the trees were thicker there. Fear began to bloom in her chest, thinking perhaps she'd wandered too far, but she dismissed it. What's the worst thing that could happen by getting in touch with nature a little?

"Caw!" the raven insisted.

"All right, all right! What's so important?" Lori laughed. She left the trail behind as she followed the raven up the hill, wondering what Conner would say when she told him the story. He'd probably shake his head and ask her not to repeat it in front of his football buddies. The raven led her all the way up the hill, insistent as ever until they reached the top.

Then it was silent.

"You finally ran out of things to say?" she asked.

But the bird wasn't looking at her anymore. It

peered down the other side of the hill, its head twitching a little to one side.

Lori looked, wondering if the raven had spotted its next snack. When she turned, she realized the two of them weren't alone. A group of people had gathered near the base of the hill on the other side. There had to be at least twenty of them. They sat around and spoke in hushed tones so Lori didn't hear anything they were saying. Given where she was in the country, Lori figured it was a hippie gathering or something. She wasn't going to bother them, but something caught her eye just as she started to turn away.

Looking back, Lori realized a dog was moving toward the group. No, not a dog. A *wolf.* It trotted up from the thicker part of the woods beyond the hill, its eyes yellow and determined. Her heart lurched in her chest. It was beautiful, the kind of thing she'd love to see up close, but it was coming right at them. Lori sucked in a breath to yell at the group, to tell them to get out of there.

But one of the men turned toward the wolf, then became one himself.

Lori blinked. That wasn't right. She hadn't just seen that. She glanced down at her fitness tracker, wondering if she'd overdone it and was now halluci-

Rex

nating. Leaning against the nearest tree for balance, Lori looked back down the hill. The man who'd been there a moment ago was gone, just as she thought, and now there were two wolves. They weren't sneaking up on the people, though. They were right there in the midst of them.

It couldn't be right, but the rest began to transform. Their faces stretched into long muzzles as their heads writhed on their shoulders. They fell forward onto all fours as thick gray fur sprouted on their bodies. Her gut twisted, but she couldn't look away. She caught glimpses of them between various forms of human and beast.

A scream ripped through the air. When the wolves all looked in her direction, she knew it was coming from her.

Lori froze, watching in horror as the pack of wolves raced up the hill. Their claws dug into the soft earth as they bounded for her, a stream of fur that moved and ran around each other without the least bit of trouble. They were gaining on her, and quickly.

"Holy shit!" Sucking in a breath, Lori scrambled back down the hill. It was steeper than she remembered it being on the way up. Her shins screamed at her to slow down. She wasn't used to all this exercise. But her brain sent an extra flood of adrenaline through her system, and she would deal with the aches and pains later.

Lori flung herself down the hill, then hit flatter land and barreled back toward the trail. She only had to get there, then someone would come along. Someone would've heard her screams and was probably on their way. Right?

She could hear the wolves, their panting breaths becoming louder by the second. She knew they had to be gaining on her, and her spine tingled in terrible anticipation. But she had to keep going. She wasn't going to give up.

Her toe caught on a root, and she pitched forward. The raven called once more as the world went black.

———

Lori slowly opened her eyes. She felt as though she'd been swimming in a deep black void for hours, and it hurt to let even the slightest bit of light in. Squinting against the painful light, Lori tried to turn her head to the side, but it hurt too much.

"Hey, there. Are you with us?" a deep voice

asked. It was rough but kind, and it sounded like it was coming from the other end of a tunnel.

She moved her mouth, trying to answer, but she didn't know how. Her mind groped around for thoughts and found none. "What... what happened?" she croaked.

"You hit your head, but you're all right now. Just take it easy." It was that same voice again, but this time it was closer.

She opened her eyes and looked up to see a rugged, handsome face. Piercing blue eyes stared down into hers, his brows wrinkled in concern. She didn't recognize him, but something within her told her she knew him.

"There you are," he said gently as she started to come to a little more. "You'll be fine."

Lori wasn't entirely sure she agreed with him.

———

More Shifter Romance Series

Beverly Hills Dragons Series

Dragons of Sin City Series

Dragons of the Darkblood Secret Society Series

Packs of the Pacific Northwest Series

Compilations

Forever Fated Mates Collection

Shifter Daddies Collection

Early Novellas

Mated By The Dragon Boss

Claimed By The Werebears of Green Tree

Bearer of Secrets

Rogue Wolf

ABOUT THE AUTHOR

Steamy shifter romance author Meg Ripley is a Seattle native who's relocated to New England. She can often be found whipping up her next tale curled up in a local coffee house with a cappuccino and her laptop.

Download *Alpha's Midlife Baby,* the steamy prequel to Meg's Fated Over Forty series, when you sign up for the Meg Ripley Insiders newsletter!

Sign up by visiting www.authormegripley.com

Connect with Meg

amazon.com/Meg-Ripley/e/B00Z8I9AXW
tiktok.com/@authormegripley
facebook.com/authormegripley
instagram.com/megripleybooks
bookbub.com/authors/meg-ripley
goodreads.com/megripley
pinterest.com/authormegripley

Printed in Great Britain
by Amazon